TAKING OUT OLD MEN

by

Elli De Ling

Copyright@2012

Edition: January 2013

ACKNOWLEDGEMENTS

Taking Out Old Men is the result of an active imagination supported by the patience and humor of my husband, Wesley Andrews. The Ann Arbor Writers Group provided suggestions and intensive edits. Hopefully, all the commas are in the right places. The cover was created by Bobbi Heldt. Alexi Rostov lives in my head and told me her story. She has other stories to tell.

TABLE OF CONTENTS

Prologue
Chapter 1 – Mackinac job
Chapter 2 – New orders – to Metro
Chapter 3 – Off to Rome
Chapter 4 – J.R. Arrives in Rome
Chapter 5 – Shaking her tail
Chapter 6 – J.R. on Palatine
Chapter 7 – Red Hat evasion
Chapter 8 – J.P. at Trevi
Chapter 9 – Tails explained
Chapter 10 – J.R. anger
Chapter 11 – Gypsies
Chapter 12 – Meet with J.R.
Chapter 13 – Not another bug!
Chapter 14 – Cardini's cover
Chapter 15 – Date with U.P.
Chapter 16 – J.P. plan – onto Alexi
Chapter 17 – Checking out the old guys
Chapter 18 – Interesting date
Chapter 19 – More investigation
Chapter 20 – On the Palatine
Chapter 21 – The mime threat
Chapter 22 – Asking Chaz a favor
Chapter 23 – J.R. at The Mask
Chapter 24 – Warnings, helping J.R.
Chapter 25 – Foiling J.P.
Chapter 26 – J.P. is S.C.
Chapter 27 – Safe House
Chapter 28 – Team Player?
Chapter 29 – To the Vatican
Chapter 30 – Last minute decision
Epilogue – Three days later

Prologue
1963

"Alexandra! Shoot!" His fist hit her back on the large bruise from her last beating, the pain sharp like a knife. Her small twelve-year old hand could barely hold the heavy old Soviet army pistol, and the muzzle wavered as she tried to point it at the rat. The gray animal looked up at her, whiskers and small nose twitching beneath round black eyes. Her finger was on the trigger. She brought her other hand up to hold the pistol steady.

"Kudoz!" He always called her a sissy. Weak, useless, no good. "Shoot!"

She sucked in a deep breath. Anger whirled her around. Alexi pulled the trigger. Her ears rang with the blast. She stumbled back with the recoil, and her right hand holding the pistol dropped to her side.

Her father lay on the floor of their small kitchen, blood spurting from his chest and pooling beneath him. His bloodshot eyes stared at the ceiling, and his mouth was open, exposing the stumps of rotten teeth. He didn't move.

Alexi let the gun fall to the floor. Her body relaxed. She didn't need to be afraid any more. She half turned and watched the rat disappear behind the stove. Someone pounded on the door. It opened and she heard footsteps. She looked up - dark brown eyes in an innocent child's oval face - saw the neighbor lady standing in the doorway to the kitchen, and smiled.

Russian immigrant families in Southfield, Michigan took care of their own. After only a week in Juvenile Hall, she was placed with the Smirnov's. They were strict and cold. They didn't trust her. She didn't call them Mom and Dad. They never talked about the father who raised her or her mother who died. She learned to obey and keep her thoughts and feelings to herself. As a Russian, she was supposed to be 'strong, like bull.' She didn't think of herself as Russian. She was American.

The week after Alexandra Petrovna Rostov graduated from Southfield High School, she left for basic Women's Army Corps training at Fort McClellan. After a tour of duty in military intelligence in Viet Nam, in 1970 she mustered out and returned to Michigan. It wasn't considered 'cool' to be patriotic in those years, and Alexi hid her rush of pride on hearing the National Anthem.

Marsdon Security in Ann Arbor hired her to provide protection for visiting dignitaries and assist in setting up security systems for corporations. From 1970 to 2006, she kept her petite body in good shape, took night courses from the company in several languages, and became proficient in self-defense and close combat skills. She wore her graying dark hair short, her Mongol ancestry evident in slightly slanting eyes and an attractive oval face. She'd never married. Had a tendency to use men sexually and toss them away. She had a basic distrust of most people, and few friends. Her one hobby was knitting complex patterned clothing, a skill she learned from her foster mother. She bought a house on the West Side of Ann Arbor and rented out an upstairs apartment to grad students.

No one ever saw her take out the picture of her real mother and curl up in bed with it and the small stuffed bear she had kept from her childhood

At age fifty-six, after a rather interesting company personality assessment; she was offered early retirement and a special lucrative contract with the company. Aging ex-assassins were losing it to senility and Alzheimer's. A patriot was needed to 'take out the old men'.

Chapter 1 - Mackinac Job
Summer, 2010

"He's the one that did in that senator last week, Alexi. Something needs to be done." Her main contact at the office was Neil Marsdon, a portly man with thinning hair. Neil had put on weight in the forty years they had worked together, and she could hear his office chair squeak as he moved around his desk.

"You are the only logical one to do this. He used to be with our government. With the agency." She knew what he meant – loyalty. The ties between Marsdon Security and government special operations were strong.

"I just got back from the last job, Neil." Her laundry was in the dryer, suitcase still open on her bed. She was standing in the bathroom stark naked, hair still dripping from a quick shower.

"The governor is on her way to Mackinac Island as we speak. I just got verification about this guy. The feds just now figured out that he killed the senator. They've got a tail on him. He booked himself to Pellston airport near Mackinaw, with a car rental waiting. The guy is losing it, 'Lexi. He even made a call to the agency to let them know that he got their message to eliminate the governor. They're going ballistic. The Midwest Governor's Conference is the only thing going on up there that would interest him. It's out on Mackinac Island."

Alexi looked at her aging self in the steamy bathroom mirror and plugged in the hair dryer with one hand. "Is the company plane available?"

"Nope. This time you take the 'copter. No time. I've already made arrangements."

"What about cleanup? Someone could identify him."

"The feds already have people on the island. They'll take care of it. You just get to him and do your thing."

Yeah. Her thing. She tried using the towel with one hand but her back was still wet. She lifted one foot and then the other to the toilet seat and dried them. Crap.

"Oh, and by the way, we've got some info on the old Cougar. The agency has been tracking him. Some rather alarming stuff came in this morning. We may need you again rather soon."

"Where?" They had been trying to get the man they called The Cougar for years.

"Probably somewhere in Europe. Daniel's working on it. So get back as soon as you can, ok?" He sounded stressed.

"Can I use the chopper to get back?"

"Yah, I'll have it waiting."

"Any idea how soon I'll have to take off again?" Soon, she hoped. It would be a real coup if she was the one to finally take the bastard out.

"Don't know yet. Thanks, 'Lexi. You're a life saver." He sounded relieved.

A life saver. What a joke. She took out her targets - not save them. Well, she saved the people they mistakenly thought they should kill. Yeah. A life saver.

At age fifty-six, Neil had looked at her rather interesting personality assessment. He offered her early retirement and a special lucrative contract with the company. Aging ex-assassins were losing it to senility and Alzheimer's. Someone was needed to 'take out the old men.'

In minutes she was on her way to the small local airport. The blades of the helicopter were already moving when she pulled up next to it.

====================

The elderly man near the end of the line of people getting on the Mackinac Island ferry didn't appear aware of Alexi standing behind him. He was carrying a long black sports bag, and went down the metal gangplank onto the boat.

She followed him up painted metal stairs to the top open deck. He walked to the rear, put his bag under the wooden seat and sat down. The wind lifted his silver hair and he unzipped his tan jacket.

Alexi passed the seats at the front of the upper deck filling with tourists. Her blue jeans, pink V-necked shirt and light blue jacket were similar to the clothing of other 'elders' on the boat.

There was a large empty space next to him. "Do you mind?" She sat down beside him without waiting for an answer and rested a big tan and white canvas bag on her lap. He pulled away, keeping space between them. No one else came to sit next to them in the back row.

"The ride sure doesn't take very long," she said. "These boats are pretty fast." The man slid a little farther away from her.

"On vacation?" she asked.

"Just a little bit of business out on the island," he answered gruffly. A group of seagulls swooped down over the dock, calling raucously. He raised his voice above the sound and asked: "How about yourself?"

"I'm on a little vacation, seeing friends." She settled back against the seat. As she leaned back, she stretched her legs out under the seat in front of them, and saw him glance at the swell of her breasts under the pink shirt.

The engine of the boat started up and drowned out conversation. As they backed away from the pier, for a moment she felt as though the pier was moving and the boat was stationary. Then they headed away from the dock, and the mainland receded behind them. The noise settled down.

"Hope you don't mind." Alexi took a piece of knitting out of her bag. "It's a sweater for my grandson. They grow so fast." She pulled the knitting needles out of a ball of blue yarn and unrolled the beginning of the back of a blue sweater.

The design was a cable stitch requiring an extra double-pointed short needle to form each cable. She took it out of her bag and shoved it into the base of the sweater.

"I don't know why I bother. He probably thinks it's kind of 'dorky' wearing a sweater knit by his grandma."

The boat sped across the water toward the island. A high white arc of water rose behind them and she felt the vibration of the engines.

She wondered why the man thought the governor had to be eliminated. The conference had been announced on television news; perhaps he had seen it. Did he think someone had ordered him to do it? Did he hear voices or imagine he got a phone call? Other old ex-CIA and KGB assassins over the years that she had 'taken out' had actually talked about it, how they got calls and messages.

Alexi knew some things about him. She read the intel in the 'copter once she was airborne. The man next to her on the ferry was responsible for so many events over the decades. Most had been a benefit to the country and its allies. But now, with his senility, he had killed a senator, and was about to again commit the unpardonable - an unauthorized assassination. He couldn't be arrested and tried. Media attention to his past would affect national security. Everything in the past might be exposed by some reporter. This was the only way.

Knowing more about the man next to her would mean getting to know him as a person. She didn't want to know him, or think about his past. He was not a person. He was a target. A dangerous target. She had seen the long black bag under the seat. Long bags often meant sniper rifles. He probably was counting on some outside activity at the conference and would aim from a distance.

Was she in danger? Probably not that much. He had always been a long range sniper. That kind was not as good up close. But she was careful.

The sun on the water sparkled, the waves low in calm water. A white frothy wake lifted as they sped toward shore. She shifted on the seat, twisting to look behind at the huge horsetail of water. Her movement brought her a bit closer to him. Then she shifted so that she was facing the island.

"Wow. The Grand Hotel! I hear that it's really elegant. Probably too pricey for me." She pointed at the long white building halfway up the hill on the island. He half turned to look.

The movement of her hand was smooth as she reached in her canvas bag and switched the short needle used to form the cables with another that was flat on one end.

It was never easy. She drew a deep breath and held the needle down at her side away from him. With her thumb she carefully pulled up the plunger. At the same time a fine steel needle slid out the other end.

It would be quick. Painless. Appear to be a heart attack. He was looking up at the seagulls, rather pointedly ignoring her, avoiding further conversation.

This was the part where she felt her father's hand on her back. The knife thrust of pain and the old Russian word 'Kudoz.' No. She was not weak. She could do it.

She noticed the thick blue veins in the back of his wrinkled hands, knowing the memory would stay with her for a while. His hands. The hands that had caused entire governments to fall, and killed a senator in Colorado a week ago.

"Oh, I think that's Bois Blanc Island!" She pointed at another island south of the larger one. He turned his head to see where she was pointing and she pushed the needle into his thigh. He jerked away and looked at her, putting his hand over the painful place.

"Oh my goodness! I'm so sorry...." She shoved the small knitting needle, now closed, into her bag. The familiar rush ran through her. What? Relief? Like killing her father again. How many times had she killed him? Not good to count. Never count.

He looked into her eyes, took a short breath, and slumped onto the seat, one hand beneath and the other curled against him.

She used her feet to slide his bag under her portion of the seat, reached down and retrieved it. Alexi stood quickly and slung her canvas bag over her shoulder. Past tourists chatting and laughing, she made her way quickly down the metal steps to the lower deck.

Alexi dropped her bags on a bench next to an open window, sat down and pulled out her cell phone. It only took a moment to send a single text number.

She thought again of the old man's hands. They had served her country and others for fifty years. His job had not been that different from hers. She would never give anyone the blue sweater. It had too many memories knitted into it.

Why was she doing this? Was she some kind of psychopathic stone-cold killer? No. Not that. It had to be done. She was a patriotic American, always. She was working for her country. If she didn't do it, someone else would. Someone had to....

She could take the next ferry back to the mainland. Take the 'copter back home. Might be enough time to get some Mackinac Island fudge.

Chapter 2 – To Metro
Two days later

Alexi got up from her glider rocker, turned off the television, and dropped her cell phone into her jeans pocket. Detroit Metro. Half hour before she had to leave for the airport. She felt a surge of excitement. Stefan Cardini - The Cougar. Her chance to get one of the really big targets.

She took a quick glance around her house. Built in 1920 on the west side of Ann Arbor, she updated it in 1990. Similar to other older frame houses on the street, it had a front porch, small front yard, large back yard, and separate garage. Like her life, the house appeared ordinary on the surface. Behind a sliding wall in the basement, it was another matter.

Yes. Barred windows closed and locked. A quick call to the grad student who lived upstairs.

"Chaz?"

"You got him." He had moved in two years ago, and was only nineteen now. The son of a woman she met at a bookstore, Chaz grew up in Ann Arbor, and graduated from Pioneer High at age fifteen. Incredibly intelligent and he had some street smarts. He had finished his bachelor's the previous year and was now nearly finished with his master's in computer science at the University of Michigan.

"I've got to be gone for a few days. Keep an eye on things."

"Right." He was engrossed in his studies and computer gaming, and could hack into anything. Useful friend, needed money, and she paid well. No hang-ups about breaking the law. "Anything special? Expecting packages?"

"No. Remember to eat and take out the garbage." He thought she set up security systems, traveled a lot. She knew she was like a second mother to him but didn't want to invade his teenage privacy and independence. "Be good."

"No!" He laughed. "You be good."

"No!" Their usual farewell.

Should she call Simon? She hadn't seen him since before she went to Mackinaw. He wanted a closer relationship, but something

---

always held her back. He was a good person. Maybe too good for her.

She picked up the new sweater she was knitting in tan, cream and brown yarn in a Fair Isle pattern and put it in a basket next to her rocker. Square pieces of intricate knitted designs she had made over the years were framed and hung on the walls of the hallway to her bedroom and bath. Recessed open shelves at the end of the hall stacked with plastic boxes contained a rainbow of colored yarns.

She applied a minimum of makeup, and checked herself out in the bathroom mirror. Innocuous as all hell. Tall, physically fit. Creamy tan complexion. Graying dark hair flipped up and out on the sides of her head. At sixty a few wrinkles and contact lenses.

What had Neil said on the phone? This was a situation where her aging target might *not* be senile. Intelligence indicated he might be working for a group of war material manufacturers strongly opposed to attempts at reconciliation between major religious groups. Yeah. Gotta keep religious wars going and the money rolling in.

She was selected primarily because of her keen ability to get close to older men. She wasn't sure whether Marsdon Security had an arrangement with the U.S. government. This job could have originated out of Interpol, or MI-6 in Britain.

So this was no old fart on a ferry boat. She needed to be prepared for any contingency. Alexi pulled her already packed suitcase out of the bathroom closet, checked its contents and rolled it out to the living room.

No plants to water, no pets. She couldn't very well be gone for weeks at a time and have anything dependent upon her. Chaz had a private entrance.

The knitting case sat on the floor next to the basket by her rocker. Everything was in place, innocent looking knitting needles lined up precisely, circular needles curled up neatly and held down with Velcro strips. Yarn and a partially finished striped sock tucked into the flap of the cover - a ball of extra heavy yarn, pair of small yarn needles - a device needed for turning heels on socks - needle end protectors - and a small pair of non-metal ceramic folding scissors. all in their respective pockets. A partially finished blue sweater requiring large needles folded neatly. The needles actually used for knitting were on top, and the special needles were under a thick flap held down by Velcro.

The needles underneath had been modified by Marsdon Security's top people, and passed even the most careful inspection at airports for the past five years. She checked her suitcase through with the knitting case inside. Plastic needles with ceramic tips that looked like plastic. Large fat ones contained parts for a plastic stun gun and pistol. Their tops unscrewed and a small button flush with the shaft was pressed to release necessary parts. Smaller needles had a sliding shaft she could pull back and use like an ice pick. Others held lethal amounts of drugs that could paralyze and kill a target. The most commonly used injection was a paralytic with potassium chloride, usually requiring only a few seconds. The circular needles with their strong plastic wire attached to the two knitting needle ends were effective as garrotes, but required strength and were only effective when approaching from behind.

Once used, most devices need reloading, although the stun gun could be recharged using her cell phone cord. The rounds for the gun were components of a necklace and bracelet in her jewelry case. Sleeves of her shirts, sweaters, jackets and blouses had special pockets for the needles, closed with small strips of Velcro.

Alexi zipped the cover shut and put it in her suitcase. Her backpack carry-on already contained her Kindle and a thin laptop computer. She grabbed her keys from the table by the door, pulled on her dark brown suede jacket, set the locks and burglar alarm, and closed the door behind her.

Always alert, she caught a slight movement of something at the back corner of her garage. She tensed and waited on the top porch step. Leaving her bags on the porch, she slipped her feet out of her shoes, held the pepper spray cylinder on her key ring with a finger on top, and walked slowly down the narrow cement walk. Alexi rounded the garage corner quickly, holding the pepper spray in front of her. She stopped and took a rapid step back.

A large skunk looked up at her with black eyes like shiny beads in its pointed face. Its feathery tail began to lift up and Alexi whirled back around the garage and up the sidewalk. A last minute odoriferous standoff wasn't in the plan. In seconds she grabbed her shoes, loaded her bags, and was on her way to the airport.

Chapter 3 - Off to Rome

Alexi followed a line of cars into long-term parking at Detroit Metro, only a few miles from the foster home where she grew up. She graduated from Southfield High, and but left for Fort McClellan and Women's Army Corps training weeks later. After a tour of duty in military intelligence in Viet Nam in 1970, she mustered out and returned to Michigan. Marsdon Security hired her to provide protection for visiting dignitaries and set up security systems for corporations, and she moved to Ann Arbor. She was living only a stone's throw from Southfield, but her foster parents now lived in Florida.

Long-term parking was only partially full. Alexi pulled her small suitcase behind her, backpack slung over her shoulder by its strong leather strap. She looked like hundreds of other travelers in the busy airport.

At the ticket counter, she picked up her boarding pass. "Can I take my suitcase here on board? It's the required size." She paid the extra fee with cash.

The airport restaurant was busy, but she found a small table. Alexi never liked waiting. She pulled out her Kindle and tried to read. Too hyped up. Forget it. She put it back. The pay for her last job - Daniel had better have proof of deposit. He tended to forget small things, like her getting paid. She looked around. No Daniel yet.

A slim full-busted waitress came to her table. She ordered for herself and Daniel. Coffees black. It might be a good idea to eat something. "I'll have anything quick."

"The beef barley soup comes with sourdough bread." The waitress stood stiffly with her pencil poised and Alexi nodded.

She had just started eating when Daniel arrived. He sat down heavily, sweating, his chubby face red. He wiped his forehead with a paper napkin.

"Didn't have much time." He brushed his hand over unruly dark hair. Daniel always wore a suit that looked slept in, this one was no exception. His tie was askew. He reached over to shake her hand. His was grotty with sweat and the small flash drive remained in her hand as she drew it back. She slid the device into her jeans pocket, wiping the moisture off in the same movement.

"Just got the go-ahead," he said. "I had to pull everything together this morning. It's all here."

"How about the deposit?" Alexi smiled; wrinkles in her face making her look even more like some sweet old lady.

"All taken care of." He sighed and reached for his coffee. "Black?"

"You don't need the sugar."

"Yeah, I know." He smiled sheepishly and sipped.

The flash drive would contain an encrypted file with everything she needed - locational information, maps, photos, and background data on her target. The Cougar. She went back to finishing her soup.

Daniel reached inside his jacket for her airplane ticket and put it on the table between them. "Hope you don't mind going to Paris on short notice. The plane leaves in less than an hour, American Airlines."

"Sure. Who would mind going to Paris?" Why had he raised his voice a little? Picking up her cup, she drained the last of the coffee and looked down at the ticket - Rome. Delta Flight 230, 2:26. She had twenty minutes to make the flight. Although Daniel had said Paris, the ticket said Rome. Nearby audio surveillance. She didn't look around, but knew they were being monitored. Now what?

The waitress came over and put the bill on the table. "I'll get it," said Daniel.

Alexi got up and swung her backpack over her shoulder, picked up her suitcase and nodded. "Catch ya later." He stayed at the table, pudgy hands cradling his cup.

She walked by a blonde woman sitting by the window, apparently inspecting her makeup in a small mirror. An obvious hearing aid was in one delicate ear, partially hidden by long blonde hair. Alexi's hearing devices were tiny and fitted inside her ear without being seen. She smiled a bit smugly and left the restaurant.

Damn, she hated being followed. No way to evade someone in a goddam airport, either. Alexi wheeled her carry-on into the nearest women's bathroom, waited until the two other women in the bathroom left, and went into the larger handicapped stall. She pulled down her jeans and underpants, taking advantage of the opportunity to pee.

The ticket for Rome matched one of her sets of I.D. She needed to switch identification and change her appearance to get past the blonde. Alexi opened her suitcase and pulled out a blonde and gray wig. The I.D. in her billfold was switched with another set. The originals she slid into a pocket inside the wig that she put on over her short hair. She put the flash drive in her backpack, stepped out of her jeans, and slipped on a long skirt, gray silky shirt and brocaded vest. Leaving on the sweater gave her a bulkier appearance. Shoes were replaced with soft moccasins. From the back of two artificial breasts in her case she removed three pieces of soft plastic, inserted one in the front of her mouth over her front teeth, and two inside her cheeks; the fake boobs were shoved in her bra. Jeans and jacket went in the carry-on. A quick change of earrings, blue contacts and a bit of blue eye shadow and she was done.

Alexi zipped up the bags, stepped out of the toilet stall, and checked herself in the mirror. A slim gray haired woman with brown eyes and soft clothing had entered. The woman in the mirror looked heavier and younger. She reached in a pocket of the vest, took out a pair of folding clear glasses and put them on.

She checked her watch. Fifteen minutes before her plane left. She put her backpack on top of her bag, and pulled it past the blonde woman who was now at a news stand pretending to read a magazine. She went through the security machine without incident but her luggage was opened and checked. She was patted down by a tired looking female officer who opened the knitting case was opened and gave it an eagle eyed once-over. The needles met the required length and no metal was in the case. It met security requirements.

Time to do the dumb grandma act. Time to get into her job persona. "I'm making some socks for my grandson," she said softly. "Trying to get them done for his birthday."

The officer smiled. "Yeah, I knit stuff myself, when I have the time. Is that the yarn that makes its own pattern?"

"Yes! It's wonderful, isn't it? I love knitting, it's so relaxing. Can't get out much usually. My son paid for this trip, it's a present." Alexi babbled on happily, and held out the ticket as if to give it to the security officer.

"No, you keep that until you get to the gate. I wouldn't try knitting on the plane, though. Not much room in those seats." The officer closed the knitting case and shoved it back in her suitcase. One of these days, some security officer would pick up on the knitting needles. Not this time.

"My plane leaves pretty soon. I hope I don't miss it!"

Alexi put her backpack on top of the suitcase, grabbed the handle and pulled it behind her. She picked up her bags and walked quickly to the counter. Most of the passengers had already boarded. Alone in the boarding tunnel for a moment, she took the opportunity to remove the wig and plastic inserts in her mouth and put them in her pocket along with the glasses. She fluffed up her flattened hair with one hand. Wearing the disguise for the long flight would be too uncomfortable.

Making it to her seat by a window, she was glad the company provided business class with its additional leg room and perks. There was no one in the seat next to her, probably arranged by Daniel. She would be able to lie down during her flight.

How many times had she gone to Rome? Perhaps a dozen. Like other large cities, it seemed to attract the type of men she was hired to follow and contact. The hotel she usually stayed in was comfortable, near the Pantheon with a local piazza with a number of good restaurants. The first couple of times it had been interesting, but she had seen most of the sights by now. It was Rome. She took out her Kindle. Apparently absorbed in her book, she was able to observe other passengers entering the plane without being noticed.

None of the passengers raised a high level of suspicion, but that didn't mean anything. One guy in a dark suit caught her eye as he went back into steerage class. He had the look of someone trying to appear ordinary. Nondescript Guy. Too ordinary. Alexi had run into enough FBI and CIA types to spot them. Although Marsdon Security staff carried out work for one branch of the federal government, there were those with other agencies and organizations that suspected Marsdon Security was performing covert operations and would love to expose them.

Thinking about missing her regular exercise regimen, she got a theraband out of her bag, looped it and slid it under her foot. Stretching her leg out and pulling up on the band, she kept it up until feeling the burn and repeated it with the other leg. Arm and shoulder exercises occupied her for the next few minutes. Her routine varied depending on the length of the flight.

Alexi got up and went to the back of the plane to use the bathroom, checking out the Nondescript Guy. He was in an aisle seat halfway back, looked up at her and quickly turned his head as if to look out the window. Must be new at the job. She suppressed a smile. On her way back to her seat, she restrained herself from accidentally bumping into him. He was young, but she could probably take him down in short order. He was probably paid to tail her.

It would be several hours before the plane landed in Amsterdam. The bulky boobs and extra shirt and vest were uncomfortable but she left them on. Too much change in appearance now might raise suspicion. Sleep would be at premium, so she drank a stiff rum and coke, curled up with the small airline pillow and blanket, and within minutes was sound asleep.

=====================

"Ma'am? Do you want anything to eat or drink?" The voice of the stewardess woke her, and she could see that it was dark outside the window. They were still in the air, but she felt rested. She stretched and looked up at the smiling uniformed woman standing next to her in the aisle.

"Yes!" She sat up and pushed the little blanket to the floor. Within minutes she had hot tea, a small breakfast of eggs and sausage, a croissant, and a covered dish of fruit. Although she preferred European breakfasts with slices of meat and cheese, it was important to keep up her strength. An American breakfast was better than nothing. She waited for the stewardess to remove her breakfast tray before going into her bag for the laptop and flash drive. She downloaded the encrypted data and flushed the flash drive down the toilet in the tiny bathroom.

For the next few hours she studied and memorized information. The target's face had undergone various permutations. Stefan Cardini was elusive, dedicated to his craft, an expert long-range sniper. After serving in the Special Forces in the Middle East in the 1960's, he worked out of Chicago as an undercover agent, with frequent jobs in Europe. He was multi-lingual, and his cover had been as an adjunct university history instructor. Apparently dealing with government bureaucracy wore him down, and he went with the best offer for his services.

The photo from 1980 showed the face of a man still handsome - a rugged face that had been scarred from an injury but partially restored with plastic surgery. A second photo taken three years ago from a distance showed a radical change. Gaunt, with dark circles under his eyes. Old facial scars were not apparent, probably due to more surgery. Used acid on his fingers – he made no prints. A man with a violent past.

Alexi had seen the results of his work. In the 1990's he murdered a high-ranking diplomat that could have made a difference in Israel and Iran. Then Cardini's elimination of an African president working with United Kingdom business interests had created serious economic fallout. Not her usual type of target. No losing it to old age. This was a man with a purpose – a skilled opponent. Unstable? No. Dangerous? Yes.

She looked up. Drink and food were carts emerging from behind the forward curtain. Time to take a break.

"I'll have tea, please."

The flight attendant was young, male and wore a continual smile that she figured had been enhanced with whitening. He brought her a prepackaged meal that was still warm. The ersatz food was palatable, and she ate without trying to identify it.

A movie started. She watched without putting on her headset. Soundless mouths opened and closed – car chases, explosions. She thought about Cardini.

He may have caused the plane crash that took a prominent politician out of the running for president in a South American country in the 1990's. It was certain that he caused the bombing of a restaurant in Geneva where world leaders were meeting to discuss solutions to problems in the Balkans. Whoever he worked for certainly had an interest in keeping factions at each other's throats. Religious fanatics? No. Arms manufacturers? More likely.

The flight attendant interrupted her thoughts as the plane came into the Amsterdam airport. "How was your flight, Ma'am?"

"Just peachy keen, thanks." Alexi smiled, started collecting her things. She would finish going over the matter of the Cougar in the hotel.

The seat belt sign was on. They were coming into Amsterdam. The Dutch made incredible chocolate. Just enough time to stop in that store in the airport before she caught her plane to Rome.

Pulling her bag with the backpack on top behind her, she regretted her bulky clothing. She walked slowly on purpose, and saw Nondescript Guy stop and pretend to tie his shoe so that he could remain behind her.

Chapter 4 - JR arrives in Rome

"Hey, watch it, old man!" The kid with a heavy black leather backpack swerved to get out of his way, but the backpack hit him on one arm and nearly knocked him down. He wasn't paying attention again and should have realized with all these college kids coming into Rome, any older person would just be seen as dirt. The kid didn't realize, of course, that he could not only disable but probably kill him with only one movement – maybe. He had been ill for a long time now. Probably not.

Another young man reached out to help him, but Jim Russell brushed off the hand. Damn kids. He didn't need their help, either. The flight from New York had been tiring, but he was sure he could accomplish what he intended in Rome.

It wasn't worth it to get mad at that kid. Nothing much was any more. With the last diagnosis knowing that he had only months or perhaps weeks to live, what did it matter? Only a year ago, he would have accepted a challenge from some young punk. He had thought he would live longer, and checking out at age seventy-two didn't seem quite fair. But then, what is fair? He had learned to live with the pain. Just one more thing to tend to and he would do it. Save his strength for that.

Russell rested at a coffee shop before collecting his bags. His left hand trembled as he lifted the cup, and he switched to his right. No point in pushing it. He had things to do and so little time.

"Coffee. Black." His voice was raspy from the old throat injury. The waitress waited with her pencil poised. "That's it."

She came back with a cup of coffee. "Are you arriving or departing?" Her accent was pronounced.

"Arriving."

"Enjoy your stay."

Right. He'd enjoy it all right. Finishing. Finally. An end to it. And to him. He smiled and the scars pulled his face into a grimace. He could feel the tightness. The waitress smiled back, but he saw pity in her eyes. He looked down at his cup. Hated it when people reacted like that. Didn't need their damn pity. He lifted the cup with his good hand and inhaled the solid aroma, sipped and found that it wasn't half bad. Felt himself relax.

He'd had a full life. Attended the best universities and at first planned a career as a research historian. But when the Viet Nam war started, he enlisted and ended up spending years in the military, eventually in Special Forces. After an injury in Bosnia, he took the medical discharge. Still functional, but not good enough for the military. Back into the world of academia.

Russell took another swallow of the coffee. Stretched his legs out under the table. Yeah, those were probably the best years.

For the first year he taught two courses in history at a college in Chicago and worked part-time for one of the most powerful men in the world as a security guard and assistant. Special assignments were a challenge. He left teaching to be available at all times to travel with the man to different countries. His employer was an avid collector of absurdly expensive ethnic art objects. He had to arrange for and supervise transport, deal with customs, avoid paying exorbitant taxes, and occasionally deal with persons who had obtained the objects by theft. Sometimes the bribes he had to pay were larger than the cost of the object.

The work itself was a challenge, as was his employer's propensity to drink large amounts of local liquor and shout at anyone who didn't understand English as though by volume alone he could provide translation. He also worked on his own special project in his spare time - one that had deep roots in his own past. An occasional contract job with one of his employer's associates and careful investments added to his growing wealth.

Just thinking about what he would have done with that money made his face lift on one side in his approximation of a smile. And what he would do in Rome. Yes.

His assets now were in a safe deposit box in New York City. His employer had died four weeks ago and Jim had donated the art collection to a museum. Jim's inheritance from his employer was substantial, but he donated the entire amount to a fund that compensated victims of child abuse.

He turned to look out at the concourse, but the wall next to him was mirrored. The same old face, wrinkled with dark circles under his eyes. His hair was completely white now, and he tried to keep it styled, thanking his genes for still having any hair at all. If he had opted for chemo, it would have fallen out, but he saw no point in prolonging the inevitable. It was a decent face that showed wear and tear, and he still had his own teeth - at least most of them were his own. His eyesight was remarkable after his cataract surgery and lens implants.

Not bad. Except for the fact that the leukemia had finally set in with no chance of remission. He picked up his bag and walked out of the airport, hoping that there would be no problem checking into his hotel. He needed a good nap.

He wanted to complete his goal before he had to check out of this life. He had access to the Vatican. The helpful people in the archives were unaware of what he was really there to accomplish.

Chapter 5 - Shaking her tail

The link in Amsterdam meant a mad dash for her next plane, but Alexi managed to get some euros, and whip into a chocolate shop to buy one piece of her favorite Dutch chocolate candy. Ate it. No point in tempting fate on the next flight. She arrived at the departure section for her flight just as people were lining up to get on, and ended up the last one seated in business class. Her wheeled suitcase was folded up quickly and put in the overhead, and the backpack went under the seat in front of her. Same procedure. Different plane.

The flight to Rome was much shorter, and she was glad that there was no seatmate to distract her from concentrating on the details about Cougar. Cardini was so much older now, and she planned the kind of image she would want to project to him if it was possible to get close.

She was slightly stiff from the long flight into Amsterdam, and after finishing a cup of tea she pulled out a Theraband strip from her backpack and began her unobtrusive exercises.

By now the plane was well on its way to Rome, and she really needed to head to a bathroom again. She unbuckled her seat belt, reached down for her backpack and pulled it up onto the empty seat next to her, stood up and slung the strap over her shoulder. She never left her bag unattended.

Going up the aisle to the small bathrooms shared by the business and first class passengers, she saw Nondescript Guy in the last row of her section. His suit was obviously off-the-rack, a bit rumpled now. He would fit in a re-run of Lawrence Welk, one of the guys sitting in the band playing a clarinet. As she passed, he didn't look up, and she held back a grin. So obvious. So they had tracked her, after all.

When she came out of the bathroom, she caught his eye, and let her shoulder bag brush against his arm ever so slightly as she walked past. She went to her seat, took out her Kindle, put the bag back under the seat in front of her and pretended to read. She had to get rid of her tail. Who could have hired him? She only had short notice about her flight, but there they were... this dude and the blonde.

Checking into the wrong hotel, going out the back door and taking a cab to the right hotel was one option. Just letting him follow her and keeping an eye on him was another. She had to think about this. Going sight-seeing before checking into the hotel would mean schlepping her stuff around. Inconvenient. Trying to ditch him by taking a series of taxis and busses was another possibility.

It was a little like having a piece of toilet paper stuck to your shoe. A 'Kling-on.' Maybe he caught her brush-against and realized he'd been outed. Maybe he would arrange to have someone else pick up her trail and back off, giving her enough time to lose him. Crap-crap-crap. She saw the steward coming down the aisle with a pillow and motioned him over.

"May I have another cup of tea, please?"

"Certainly, ma'm." He continued on to give the pillow to someone seated behind her and went forward again. The tea was brought promptly. She was grateful for the warmth and flavor, and it gave her more time to think of a plan.

========================

The pilot announced their arrival in Rome. By the time the plane had taxied to the gate, Alexi was standing, had taken her suitcase out of the overhead and was ready with the backpack over her shoulder.

Going down the tunnel to the terminal, she rotated her shoulders and neck slightly as though working out some stiffness, turning enough to see that the Kling-on was behind her, pacing himself to her speed.

Why were they following her? Something must have been leaked. Neil should be told. This time, she wasn't up against some old guy that was losing it by himself. The thought gave her a momentary shudder. She felt her gut tighten and some of the tea came up in the back of her throat. Alexi swallowed and took a deep breath.

A small shop in the airport had a local newspaper in English and she bought one, folded it, and put it in her bag. A long row of taxis outside were picking up incoming passengers, and she took the first one.

========================

Once Alexi got herself into the taxi, she pulled out her cell phone

"Marsdon here." Neil's familiar voice.
"Alexi."
"Yo."

"Got a bit of a Velcro problem since the second lap. You need to check out any GPS on my phone."

"Did that. It's clean."

"Got a plan. May be hard to reach me. Will call back." She looked behind her and saw that another cab was following closely, but she couldn't see the occupant in the back seat.

"Yo."

She hung up. If there was any information or change in the task ahead, it would have to wait while she ditched her tail. She leaned forward and tapped the driver on the shoulder.

"Can you take a quick right at the next corner?"

He turned and smiled. "No Engleese."

"Oh, well, then just stop. I will get out."

"Stop?" He shrugged and kept going until he came to a spot where signs indicated that taxis could wait next to the curb. "Okay, lady." He pulled over and parked at the end of the line of taxis. Alexi paid the driver, adding more for a generous tip, and pulled her bags out of the car. She grabbed her bags and walked quickly to the first taxi in the line. Schlepping luggage in Rome - just what she hadn't wanted.

Leaning over to talk to the driver, she asked directions to the nearest inexpensive hotel. The driver spoke English, and went into a lengthy discourse on how he could get her there with her bags for a minimal amount.

Alexi kept up a lengthy conversation about the fare until she determined that the taxi following her had stopped next to the line of taxis and was being approached by one of the Carabineri in a black uniform.

The policeman strutted across the street, holding up his hand so that oncoming traffic stopped. He motioned for the taxi to move on out of the way, and the driver complied. The vehicle rolled slowly past the place where Alexi was standing and she straightened up in time to see her Kling-on in the back seat. He unsuccessfully tried turning his head so she wouldn't identify him.

She grinned at her departing tail, tossed her bags on the back seat, and got in.

"Ok. We go hotel now." He pulled out and made a U-turn in front of the Carabineri standing across the street. Alexi waved at him and he smiled and saluted as they drove past.

Alexi just wanted to get to a nice quiet hotel room, stash her stuff, and submit to her tea addiction. Maybe even a nap. She carried tea bags in the carry-on, and there was always hot tap water and cups or glasses in the bathroom.

She checked in quickly, pleased with the small but inviting room, a large bed with decent pillows, and the big window that looked out over the indoor patio below. She put a chair under the door handle, made sure the window was locked and made a quick check for bugs or cameras.

A few minutes with the newspaper confirmed the schedule of events at the Vatican for the next few days. She entered some data into her computer. Forget the tea, she was tired.

Alexi got undressed quickly and crawled into the bed, turning her back on the window where it was still light outside. Sleep came quickly.

========================

When Alexi woke up two hours had passed, and she felt much better. Of course, her Kling-on could have information about her hotel reservation the same way he had known what planes she was on. She decided to make one more change in location. The nap had been necessary, or she would have been running on empty, and empty at sixty was distinctly unpleasant.

Alexi dressed casually in dark slacks and a blouse, and took a sweater in case it was needed. Changing her hair to a pale blonde wig, she applied makeup and added a pair of gold earrings. Surveying the result, she decided on a change of eye color as well, and slipped in a pair of blue contacts. She still looked sixty, but it was a stylish transformation from her travel-worn waif look.

She dumped the contents of her carry-on suitcase onto the bed, and retrieved the most essential items that would go in the backpack that would stay with her at all times. The knitting needle case, thin computer, cell phone, pouch with odds and ends, her small purse. Wigs, disguise items and makeup were included in a small black leather bag that had been rolled up in the bottom of the suitcase. Only the most innocuous items and clothing were left in the suitcase in the event that she had to leave it behind.

Hoping that her appearance had changed enough to at least slow down the Kling-on, she checked the room once, drank lukewarm tea and slipped the plastic hotel glass in her suitcase. Alexi left the room key on the dresser where it would be found in the morning, and used a bathroom towel to wipe down any fingerprints. She used the hem of her blouse to turn the door handle and exit the room, wiped the outside door handle, and any surface she might have touched on entering. It was probably a futile exercise, but it was her standard procedure and might slow things down a bit.

Instead of taking the elevator, she found the service stairway used by the maids and other hotel staff, and walked down to a hallway leading to an outside door. The alley outside had garbage containers lining one side and parked cars on the other. High cement and brick walls stretched up overhead. Cats were abundant, each guarding their own territory, consisting primarily of cars parked in the alley. Avoiding any feline-human conversation that would gain her a furry attachment, she walked quickly to the busy street at the end and took a quick left away from the hotel.

Finding a taxi proved to be easy. The driver was competent, traffic fairly light, and the usual number of motorbikes and scooters assured that any following taxi would be spotted immediately.

Alexi asked to be let out at one of the larger piazzas, carried her bags across the street and went into a women's clothing store.

Pretending to examine a rack of blouses near the front window, she checked to see if there was any evidence that she was still being followed. Everyone going past the window seemed to be busy with their own concerns. One older man looked in the window at her and smiled, revealing a single missing eye tooth. She smiled back.

Just as a woman wearing a store name tag started toward her, Alexi turned and headed for the door. She exited before having to explain herself, and continued down the street. The suitcase was getting heavy, and she needed a new hotel.

A taxi was coming toward her, and she flagged it down. The driver jumped out, grabbed her suitcase and tossed it into the back seat before she could make a move. He spoke some English, pegging her immediately for an American. Finding another hotel near the Pantheon was not difficult, but this time she chose one that was smaller and more exclusive, with a double entry system and a man at the desk 24/7. She picked up an old fashioned heavy key to her room and made her way through a maze of small hallways past a well-appointed breakfast room to a tiny elevator.

This room was on one of the top floors, with a large window that swung out. It faced a light gray painted wall which apparently was another building. She looked down at a considerable drop to the alley below. There didn't appear to be any way someone could enter her room from outside, unless they came down from the roof. She looked up and saw an overhang one story above her. Yes. That way. She pulled the window shut, locked it, and turned on the fan below the window.

Alexi went through the routine - her small device from the base of her hair dryer that she used to check the room for bugs and cameras just in case her followers anticipated her movements. Nothing. Then she sat down on the bed and laughed at herself. Paranoia had evidently set in. Although she had experienced this before, it seemed as though her tails were more astute than usual. How the hell had they got onto her so fast? Why would they think that she required surveillance?

Her basic distrust of most people sometimes increased the paranoia. Her home was protected in many ways that a casual observer wouldn't notice. Even the upstairs apartment she rented out to Chaz had extra security, not that he ever remembered to set the alarm system.

Alexi set up her toilet articles in the bathroom and put on a one-size-fits-all sleeping shirt with a picture of a dolphin on the front.

She turned on the television to CNN, changed the language from Italian to English, propped pillows up against the headboard of the bed. and settled in. Time to go over the material on the Cougar one more time. She took notes in her own shorthand code on the laptop with locational data set up on a chart that could be expanded and checked off once she had covered the various possible sites where Cougar could be found. She began prioritizing the places where he had been seen by frequency and dates. His possible disguises were also recorded in a separate file, habits and personal preferences in another. She compressed all the files into a single folder, slipped in a flash drive and recorded the folder. The flash drive went into her knitting bag. Although all of her material was encrypted, she believed in redundancy.

It was getting close to evening, and shadows had appeared on the wall opposite her window. She picked up the telephone. No restaurant in the hotel. They served only breakfast until around 11 a.m., but there was a good restaurant next door.

Alexi dressed casually, put on the blonde and gray wig, and inserted blue contacts. With her backpack again slung over one shoulder, she wound her way through the small hallways to the street. The restaurant was on her left, a few diners already seated at candle-lit tables. It seemed like a reasonable choice for dinner and she went in the front double door, up a small set of steps, and stood inside the second set of doors. A waiter came over immediately, wearing a long white apron and a big smile.

"One for dinner?" His English was excellent, and she was somewhat relieved. If she didn't know what exactly was on the menu, here was someone who might be able to assist.

Her Italian was rudimentary at best. Of course, in Rome, there were so many people who spoke English that it was simply not a problem.

With the waiter's assistance, she ordered *Filetti de Trota in Salsa di Finocchio* - trout fillets in fennel sauce. He suggested the cold sweet-and-sour eggplant to go with it, and she agreed. If she had room afterward, she wanted to try the hazelnut cake with whipped cream. Her one indulgence on trips was enjoying good food.

It was never good to have only one way to get out of a place. Alexi asked directions to the ladies room and wended her way past the kitchen to a small staircase that led to the basement. The bathrooms were at the end of a small hallway, and there was an exit door to the outside. She opened it just a crack and saw a small narrow set of cement steps leading upward to the alley that was probably just under the window of her room. Good to know. Just in case.

A small glass of white wine was served with the trout, and she ordered coffee after she finished eating. She didn't have room for the cake, but drank excellent hazelnut flavored coffee.

Paying her bill, she went out the double entrance doors and turned right to go back to her hotel when she saw the male Kling-on standing across the street, pretending to read something that looked like a street map from the light of a store window. Good grief! Would they never give up? She wondered if they got a position on her from her cell phone somehow. Probably. She had mentioned it to Neil. Damn.

Ignoring him, she went back to her hotel room. Everything appeared to be untouched, but she had left nothing inside that would help their inspection anyway. She made sure the window and door were locked, ran her electronic check for bugs again and didn't find any, and re-checked for any surveillance cameras near the ceiling. The last thing she needed was a Kling-on seeing her prancing around in her aging altogether.

To hell with it. Alexi was more than tired. She pulled the drapes across the window, got back into her nightgown, put on a pair of bed socks, brushed her teeth, put on her reading glasses and settled into bed with her Kindle. In minutes, she was sleepy, put the Kindle and glasses on the stand next to the bed, turned off the light, and was asleep.

Chapter 6 – JR on the Palatine

Jim Russell sat on the bench in the small overgrown garden on Palatine Hill watching small birds flutter back and forth from the ground to a cedar tree. The climb up to his favorite spot had winded him, but what didn't these days? It seemed as though his body was gradually disappearing. From various surgeries over the years, some associated with his employment, he felt as though he had left body parts strewn behind him on the road of life. The bottles of medication now filled a large portion of one of his bags at the hotel.

After he arrived in Rome, he ate a small lunch and took a short nap in his hotel room. As soon as he felt able to make the trek, he walked up the ancient stone path to the top of Palatine Hill, to enjoy an area devoid of all but a few hardy visitors.

Jim stretched his arms out along the back of the bench. The sky above was clear blue. He was surrounded by vegetation that had grown here for thousands of years. Perfect for what he had planned. He could hear the traffic rushing below him on the busy streets. It was easy to imagine the horses and donkey carts that were a part of old Rome.

He loved this place, and when he was in the ancient city, he often wandered among the remains of homes where the elite had lived - ruins of volcanic tufa and crumbling plaster. Reconstructions and the museum had been built to tell their stories. There was only a small exhibit of the really ancient occupants of the Palatine. Always a reflection of who was in power, the museum was a testament to the builders of the city and its place as a major player in the development of Western civilization. They nearly ignored the pagan beliefs, so immersed in Christianity. Damn statues of their saints. Damn priests and nuns – they were everywhere.

He ran a hand through his white hair, stretched, and tried to work out the kinks in his back and shoulders. His legs seemed to be working fairly well today. It would soon be time to get something to eat, as blood sugar level was always a task to be attended to.

Any weeks in Rome were precious, and he wanted to remain in good shape. He had to complete the job.

His trip back down the hill was easier than the trek up. He caught a bus to his hotel. The breakfast room was still open, and he stopped in for a quick snack of fruit and yogurt before going to his room.

Lying on his bed, he watched CNN, not bothering to change the language to English. The upcoming meeting of religious leaders would have a strong impact on world economy. When the Vatican bishop came on the program to discuss the Catholic church's involvement in organizing the meeting, he felt his hatred of the man and everything he stood for, and let out a loud expletive. "Bastards! Fucking holier-than-thou assholes!"

Chapter 7 - Red Hat evasion

One of the best things about working on contract was setting her own hours. She flung her arms above her head, stretched her legs as far as they'd reach toward the bottom of the bed, and then did her bicycle exercise for a few minutes.

Breakfast in the little room downstairs was a delight. Slices of semi-hard cheeses, prosciutto, crusty bread with butter, and a cup of Earl Grey tea. There were other people in the room, mostly couples engrossed in conversation in several languages. Alexi wore the blonde wig and blue contacts, a dark pants suit with her gray blouse, small gold earrings, low shoes, and her inevitable black backpack. She should blend in with others in the busy city.

After breakfast she checked her room. Anyone in it since she left? Everything appeared untouched. The guy tailing her would probably wait until she left the hotel for the day. Downstairs at the desk, she rang the small bell for the concierge.

"Yes? May I help you, madam?" He was a tall, thin young man in a dark blue suit, his white shirt a contrast against his tanned complexion. His silvery gray tie was carefully knotted, his shoes polished and his smile a testament to tooth-whitening.

Alexi smiled. "Are there any messages for me?" She gave him her room number, and he checked on a computer at the desk.

"Nothing, madam."

"Thank you."

"I'm going out for the day now."

"Yes, madam. Be careful of the gypsies. They steal from your pockets."

"Yes, I know." Actually, she had spent a wonderful day with a group of gypsies in Athens, Greece on another job without anyone stealing anything. Far from it.

Alexi found the weather outside near perfection, and was glad she had put her sweater in the bag instead of wearing it. Three taxis were parked on the street outside the hotel, and she went to the one in front.

"Piazza Navona, please." The driver nodded, but didn't try to strike up a conversation. She relaxed back against the seat and enjoyed the ride through the ancient city, marveling at the way the old and new were blended in a pleasing combination. The Carabineri were everywhere in their black, red and white uniforms. She saw two of the policemen on horseback, wearing long capes.

Alexi turned to look out the back window and saw another taxi following closely. She needed to lose the Kling-on before tracking down the Cougar. A large tour bus pulled in just ahead of her taxi, and although the motor scooters and bicycles were able to get past it, her driver seemed to be stuck in follow mode. She leaned back, not bothering to think about it. They would get there when they got there.

She paid the driver, slung her backpack over her shoulder, and looked across the piazza to plan her next move. The Cougar had been seen here as an early morning regular. Many shops and restaurants ringed the large rectangular piazza. Huge fountains with statues and flowing water were impressive, as were the ornate carvings and sculptures on the surrounding buildings.

Artists had set up their tables and displays under bright awnings on either side of the piazza, and shoppers went from one to the other. A few artists sat on folding chairs at their displays, and some had small stoves for heating tea or coffee, cradling their cups in their hands as they waited for paying customers.

The restaurants around the piazza had tables outside under awnings, and a few people were already seated with morning coffee and breakfast. The sun had risen just over the tops of the buildings, and shadows created by the angle of sunlight made the scene even more picturesque than it would be later in the day.

Alexi wandered from one display to another, looked over the paintings, and finally settled on a small one of a scene of Venice painted in an old style. The artist grinned showing several missing teeth, and took her Euros gratefully. He rolled the painting, put rubber bands around it, rolled it again in newspaper and slipped it into a plastic tube. Alexi put it in her shoulder bag. Anything larger would have been difficult to take home.

As she arranged her purchase, she half turned and saw the Kling-on a few stalls behind her. This wasn't working very well. She looked around and saw several white haired men. She needed to get close enough to them to determine if one was her target. She tried to hide her irritation as she went from stall to stall, pretending to be interested in the displayed artwork. So far, none of the men appeared to be the Cougar. There were a few white haired men sitting at tables outside the restaurants, and she wandered past at a leisurely pace, pretending to check out the posted menus. None of the men fit the description.

The man following her stayed back but seemed to be having some trouble being unobtrusive. He didn't seem to know what to do with himself. He looked at the paintings, but every time she moved, he did as well. Good grief. Alexi felt her irritation escalate to a new height. If he kept this up, she might have to take him out. She didn't take out young men. Crap-crap-crap.

A tour bus pulled up next to the piazza, and a group of older women got out, chatting and laughing, wearing red hats of various shapes, some with red feather boas, and many in red and purple jackets and clothing. A Red Hat Club! Alexi grinned. She had seen them at home, and couldn't imagine belonging to anything so silly. But they did seem to have a great time, and had wonderful attitudes about growing older.

The group started to come toward her, and Alexi moved on, not wanting to be identified as an American or a potential member of anything as ridiculous as the Red Hat Club. And yet... She went diagonally across the piazza toward one of the restaurants with outdoor seating and a shop with a multitude of cheap tourist items next to it.

Alexi slipped into the shop and found a hat display. Yes. A red hat. Bright, red, and large. Made of some kind of fake plastic straw with a large red silk rose attached to one side. Perfect. It could be rolled up and shoved in her bag. To complete the outfit, she found a red scarf hanging from a rack. She paid for her purchases, put the plastic bag with the hat and scarf in her backpack and wound her way through a maze of outside souvenir racks to the restaurant next door.

Sitting at one of the outside tables, she spotted her King-on coming across the piazza. He went to the restaurant next to the one where she was sitting and took a seat at an outside table where he could see her.

Alexi ordered tea, a croissant, and a bit of cheese. She took out her Kindle and pretended to read as she ate. After half finishing the food, she left euros on the table under a paper napkin. She slid the hat and scarf out of the plastic bag inside her purse, pulled out the empty bag and laid it on the table.

The waiter came to her table with the check. "Would you like more tea, ma'am?"

"Yes, thank you. Where is the lavatory?"

The waiter pointed, and she got up, taking her bag with her. Damn. She would have liked another cup of tea. Shit. She had to get rid of the tail.

In the bathroom stall, she reversed her suit jacket so that it was now a light tan, took off the blonde wig, and put on the red hat and scarf. A short hallway went directly out to the piazza.

A group of the crimson-hatted women moved around the piazza like a flock of birds, chattering and laughing. They bought paintings and art objects, stuffing them in identical large pink shopping bags. One of the ladies appeared to be the leader. She talked and gestured at the front of the group, and sometimes walked backwards so they could all see her. Alexi was concerned, as the woman looked as though she had seen age 70 some years ago and might trip and fall over backward on the cobblestones. But she managed to not only keep her balance but seemed to be saying amusing things that made the group burst out laughing. The whole thing was like watching a situation comedy on television with an ongoing laugh track.

Alexi followed the festooned women. Several swept into a tourist shop and she trailed behind them, moving with a smaller group of five women that went back outside and headed for the outside tables of a nearby restaurant. They sat down and Alexi came to them. She stood by their table, biting her lower lip nervously.

"Do you mind?" she asked.

"Hey, whadda ya know! We got us a new member!" The woman who was the head of the group shifted in her chair and looked up at Alexi, a broad smile revealing what was obviously an expensive set of false teeth. "Siddown, gal! Take a load off! Where ya from?"

"Ohio! Toledo, Ohio!" Alexi grinned, posing with the hat for the woman. "How's this?" She took a chair at the table.

"Great!"

Two other women looked at Alexi and smiled with a bit less enthusiasm. They didn't appear to be too happy to have an outsider join their group.

"Where are you from?" Alexi asked.

The woman adjusted her boa. "N'Orluns, honey. Loo-zee-ah-nah."

"So where are you going today?"

"Vatican museum. The Pope is supposed to be doing his blessings later in the week. Gonna go to that. We could use it!" The boa was readjusted, and the hat.

"Mind if I tag along? I can pay the bus fare, if that's required. I'm here on my own, my girlfriend got sick at the last minute, had to have her gall bladder out, and I already had my ticket..." Alexi looked semi-serious, but under the red hat and scarf, she knew she didn't appear too grief-stricken at her girlfriend's illness.

"Sure, honey. Just blend in with us and the bus driver won't know the difference. But we gotta get goin' pretty soon if we want to see anythin' else."

Alexi kept her back to the piazza, hoping the Kling-on wouldn't recognize her, and kept up an easy banter with the women in her new persona until they all finished their coffee break. She tried to hide her irritation at her situation. She needed to shake the tail and focus on the job.

The leader got up, went out in front of the restaurant and pulled a little red whistle on a red string out of ample breastworks covered in a fuzzy red sweater. Her tight purple pants held in a considerable amount of thigh and belly, but she was wearing sensible pink walking shoes.

She blew the whistle and Red Hat ladies came running, boas trailing behind them, hats flapping, and the mass of pink, red, and purple was a whirl of color in the otherwise somewhat sedate piazza. Alexi managed to get herself into the center of the group, hoping that her pants suit would blend in enough that she wouldn't be spotted.

An older woman without a red hat walked by the group - a short gray-haired person with an interesting purse made out of a large powder horn, the kind used to load gunpowder into muzzle-loaded guns in past centuries. The woman looked her way for a moment, winked, grinned, and turned away. Curious.

The group made its way across the cobblestone piazza to the tour bus, and Alexi looked straight ahead, not trying to make any small talk until she got on the bus. She saw the Kling-on looking at the group and then at the table where she had been sitting. If he had identified her, he would probably find a taxi and follow the bus, but she had other plans for that situation.

"Well, you just come and sit by me, honey." The leader had saved Alexi a spot next to her just behind the bus driver. "Now, I'm Veronica. What's your name again?"

"Judy. Judy Mayhew."

"Judy Mayhew from Toledo, Ohio. My, my. Well, I'm glad to meet 'cha." Veronica stuck out her hand. Her nails were long and painted a bright red. She took off her hat and Alexi could see thinning hair with shiny bits of scalp through the wisps of gray. The false teeth clicked a little bit when Veronica spoke. She adjusted the red feathery boa again, and then pulled it off and made it into a soft pile on her lap.

"I'm really happy you let me come along. I was getting kind of lonesome. Guess it was sort of foolish coming here all by myself, but I already had the ticket..." Alexi looked over at Veronica and smiled shyly. What an act. They seemed to believe her, so what did it matter.

She realized that the woman next to her had cleared her throat and was starting to speak. Stifle it, 'Lexi. Act interested.

"We're kind of on a mission here... in a manner of speaking." Veronica looked over and lowered her voice. "Some of us isn't as well as we could be, and we kinda thought that getting the Pope's blessing..." She looked back quickly, and then her wrinkled hands clutched the feathery red boa on her lap.

"I see. That sounds like a very good reason to come to Rome!" Alexi smiled, remembering a neighbor's bout with breast cancer. The treatments, the days of waiting to find out the results of tests.

"So, here we are! Might as well do it up! That's what I allus say. Just do it up!" Veronica smiled, the false teeth slipping a little. She shoved the red hat back on her head.

Alexi adjusted her own red hat and the scarf. "Yup. Just do it up, gal!"

The ride to the Vatican didn't take long. As the tour bus pulled into a slot next to dozens of other busses, the ladies made ready to get out. Alexi looked out the window and saw thousands of folding chairs already set up and in the distance the place where the Pope would be speaking. A few small vendors were set up with souvenirs, blessed religious items for sale, pictures of the Pope on plates, and other items.

The Red Hat ladies made their way out of the bus, and Veronica stood on the sidewalk next to the bus, counting heads, with her little red whistle in her hand. Alexi waited until the ladies had exited and then made her way to the back exit. Just as Veronica blew on her whistle, Alexi slipped into the tiny bathroom in the back bus exit and pulled the door behind her quietly. Then she took off the red hat and scarf and put them in her shoulder bag.

The area around the busses was deserted, their occupants having gone on to the Vatican with tour groups. The ladies were moving down the sidewalk like a flock of birds again, and Alexi smiled as she thought of a group of cardinals. Of course, there were also Cardinals at the Vatican, and red hats... she grinned to herself, wondering what the priests thought of Red Hat ladies.

If she hadn't spoken with Veronica on the bus, she would have had a completely different view of the group. The serious side was buried under silliness, bright colors, and laughter.

Might as well just do it! The philosophy made sense, somehow.

Alexi walked away from the Vatican tours, found a side street, crossed it quickly, and went into a clothing store. She didn't see any followers, but thought it was time to do something about her phone. She selected a thin silk blouse which she took into a changing room to try on. She closed the curtain, took out her cell phone, and pried open the back.

It took a minute or so, but she located the bug that was causing her grief. No more Kling-ons! She picked off the bug, put it in her pocket, and replaced the phone in her bag. Going back out into the store, she wandered past another woman whose purse was open just slightly on one end. The bug was easily dropped into the woman's purse.

Alexi went to the front of the store, paid for the blouse. It was a really nice shade of blue, and would roll up tightly - and went out of the store. No Kling-on in sight - yet. She flagged down a taxi and gave directions to what had been her original goal. The most likely place where Cougar could be found at this time of day. If he followed his old patterns.

Chapter 8 - Meets JP at Trevi

The sun was overhead now, and Alexi walked across the street with a cluster of people, the only way to manage in a city with so few stoplights and traffic signs. Traffic was stopped both ways for the clustered bunch of people that half-skittered across the cobblestones focused on simply getting to the other curb and sidewalk. The old saying about crossing streets in Rome was probably true, either you were quick or you were dead. Or was that just a movie title? She couldn't remember. Too much stuff had gone into her brain in 60 years, and sometimes it wasn't worth sorting it out.

She noticed a few cats sitting regally on the bases of statues in the square, and smiled as she remembered the 'Cats of Rome' calendar hanging in her kitchen. They seemed well fed and content. The ones in the alley next to her hotel each seemed to have their own area. She had seen dishes in alley doorways that were obviously food and water dishes for the cats. They were everywhere.

The Trevi Fountain was busy, as usual, with tourists taking pictures and tossing coins in to make wishes. A few Carabineri were in evidence, but they stayed primarily under awnings in the shade rather than out in the bright sunshine. The temperature had definitely risen since early morning. Alexi wondered if the uniforms were uncomfortable in warm weather.

At a restaurant near the fountain she took a seat at a table, took out her knitting and started working with her non-lethal needles on the striped sock, pleased as the design appeared almost magically with the self-patterning yarn. She had already finished the ribbing and was knitting the tube below it on three needles. It would be a while before she needed to concentrate on turning the heel, and she used the activity to cover her real intent - to see if the Cougar would make an appearance. The information had said that this was one of his regular places to visit.

"Does madam want something to drink?" The waiter was standing next to her, and she cursed herself at not being adequately aware of her surroundings, focused instead on the piazza.

"Yes, please. Bottled water." She put her knitting on the table and took the offered menu.

"Gas? No gas?" he asked.

"Gas, please." She loved the Italian carbonated water and often bought it to drink at home, but in Rome it was much less expensive.

"Something to eat?"

"Not right now, perhaps later." She laid the menu on the table and picked up her knitting.

The waiter left, and she resumed her casual surveillance of the area near the fountain. A few older persons drifted past, primarily women with younger people, perhaps their families, but no single older man.

A group of Asian tourists came marching down the sidewalk to her left, past the ornate buildings that ringed the fountain area. The person in front was wearing a bright pink vest and holding a bright pink bike flag held high over his head. Every person in the group was wearing a bright pink vest to match. Most of them wore backpacks, and had cameras hanging around their necks. The kind of cloth hats that Alexi's father had worn fishing. She remembered a sheep herder she had seen once in the American west. 'Poor sheep,' she thought to herself, smiling. Hopefully, the closest she would come to taking a tour was her experience with the Red Hat ladies.

Alexi had been knitting, drinking the 'water with gas,' and having a not-much-needed snack of bread and cheese for nearly an hour before she saw a tall white-haired man wearing a dark suit approach the fountain. He stood there quietly for a minute and then reached in his pocket and tossed a coin into the water. Only a few tourists were close by, and he appeared to be alone. She sat up straighter and rotated her head as if to exercise a stiff neck. With the movement, she turned so that she had a better view. It could be him. The Cougar. According to her intel, this had been his pattern, at the Trevi.

He walked away from the fountain after a few minutes, and headed toward the same restaurant where Alexi was sitting. She resumed her knitting, hoping to get a closer look at his face, and was surprised when he walked up to the podium where a waiter was already standing to guide him to a table. She could hear the conversation easily as she was only sitting a few feet away.

"Welcome, sir. Do you wish to have lunch?" The waiter glanced over at Alexi, perhaps thinking she had been waiting for this person, but since she didn't give any sign of recognition, he gestured for the man to follow him to a table some distance away from her.

Her glass had been refilled several times, and she needed to go to the bathroom, which was conveniently just past the white haired man.

She laid her knitting on the table, stood and picked up her bag. He looked up and she caught his eye and smiled. Not too much. Just a little flirty. Looked away.

He picked up his wine glass and raised it to her like a toast. She bit her bottom lip and ducked her head shyly. He turned back to reading what appeared to be an Italian newspaper. The small camera in the shoulder strap only needed a quick slide of her thumb and the man's image was recorded.

He fit the description of the Cougar, with his white hair and general appearance, but was in much better shape than she had expected. This man's face may have been altered with plastic surgery, but it was not immediately apparent. He was wearing an expensive tailored suit, white shirt, and dark gray tie. He glanced up at her as she passed his table, smiled slightly, and looked back at his newspaper.

Alexi hoped she wasn't too blatant with her aging 'Princess Di' glance at him (head lowered, looking up shyly through her lashes) as she walked past him. After she returned to her table and noticed that the waiter had placed a glass of red wine on her place mat.

"Oh, sir?" She waved her arm over her head, and the waiter came immediately. "I didn't order the wine." Alexi pretended to look perturbed and a bit put out by the intrusion.

"The gentleman over there..." the waiter said.

"Well, thank him, but I must decline. Please bring me the bill." Alexi stood up, acting flustered by the attention. She put her knitting in her backpack.

"Of course, madam." The waiter went back into the restaurant, leaving Alexi standing with her backpack clutched tightly to her side, wearing an irritated expression.

The white haired man stood up and walked over to her. "I am very sorry if I've offended you. Please accept my apology." His voice was rather deep, with a bit of a British accent, and the expression in his dark eyes seemed sincere.

"Oh, oh... well, I'm not in the habit of... I'm not sure what..." Alexi was actually a bit flustered by the situation. She hadn't expected to make any contact with her target - or a person who might turn out to be her target - quite so soon. Certainly not this directly.

"You were sitting by yourself, and I thought maybe you would like someone to talk with..." Now it was the man who seemed uncomfortable. His eyes were a light brown, and he looked directly at her. She felt herself drawn to him somewhat, but kept up her guard.

"Oh, my... Well... I don't know... I've never done ...." She stood clutching her bag, looking around as if hoping for some kind of guidance. She needed to let him think he was in control, and the clueless tourist was as good as any ruse.

"That's all right. Perhaps tomorrow. I come here every day around this time. You may change your mind." He smiled and she noticed that he apparently had his own teeth - and hair - which was remarkable. He also had kept his weight down. Actually, if she wasn't going to have to kill him...

"Perhaps... Oh my, I do have to be going." The waiter brought her bill and she paid him, including a sizeable tip. She started to walk away, and then turned around as though changing her mind.

"Oh, I'm Elaine. Elaine Birdsall - from Michigan. U.S.A." She gave him a half smile, in what she hoped was a close imitation of an aging secretary from the United States, thinking about picking up a man in Rome.

"Joe Pelloni – Bloomington, Indiana. U.S.A. Practically neighbors." He grinned. "Don't let the English accent fool you. I just spent some time in London and it stuck."

"But you're reading an Italian newspaper...." She looked up at him again.

"Oh, my folks are Italian. Learned from my grandma, stayed summers on her farm." He grinned again. "So can we meet again tomorrow?"

"Well. I don't know." Alexi hesitated as though turning it over in her mind. "What the heck. I guess. I mean this is pretty public." She looked around the nearly empty outdoor restaurant area. "Okay, I'll be here."

He looked at his watch. "One o'clock? Perhaps for lunch?"

She nodded her head, trying for 'shy acceptance.' She walked away from the restaurant looking straight ahead. Don't look back at him. Charming, but perhaps also her target - Joe Pelloni from Indiana.

Chapter 9 - Tails explained

Alexi went through the double entry into her hotel. The young concierge was still at the desk. He smiled as he recognized her. She waved her hand slightly - was it one of those Queen Elizabeth waves? Perhaps. Good grief. Princess Diana-on-Metamucil and a Q.E. wave all in one day. Europe must have an effect on her. She went to the elevator and was glad that it was only minutes before she could have a nice cup of tea and a bit of a rest.

The water from the tap was hot enough for a cup of Earl Grey, and she opened the drape, unlatched the window and swung it open. The air outside was cool and refreshing.

Sitting on the edge of her bed, the tea on the nightstand within reach, she took out her cell phone and called the office in Ann Arbor, remembering the time difference and hoping that someone would be there. By now, they should have changed the satellite and she shouldn't be tracked on GPS. The matter of the bug in the phone puzzled her as the phone was one Neil had assured her was clean and had never been out of her possession. How did the device get planted?

Neil picked up on the first ring. "Marsdon here."

"Hey, Roma here."

"Yo."

"Question. Had a bug in the phone. Ditched it. How'd it get there?" She picked up the tea and took a sip.

"Planted by us. Training exercise."

"What?" She sat up straighter, feeling anger rising like a wave inside her.

"The guy tailing you - your piece of Velcro - was in training. With us."

"No shit." She took another sip of tea, more of a gulp this time.

"New guy. Trying him out. He ended up following someone down to Sorrento. He's still there. Not too good at driving, either. Kinda dinged up the rental." Alexi could hear amusement in Neil's voice.

"Huh." She took another sip of tea.

"You did a good ditch, Roma." Neil paused, and then continued. "The bit with the Red Hat ladies was a hoot. He got it on camera."

Alexi imagined the office staff privy to that sort of thing watching the video of her escapade with the gaggle of fluttering women. She groaned and then smiled. "Well, I do try." The wave of irritation subsided some, but not much.

"You done good." Alexi could hear Neil shifting in his chair. He sometimes winced from a back problem

"Thanks." Praise from Neil was rare, and she appreciated it. "So do I still have Velcro?"

"Nope."

"What about the trainee?"

"He's gonna do shit work in the office. Might have to let him go."

"Too bad. He can kinda blend in to the woodwork, but I'd lose the 50's look."

"That and other things." Neil sounded as though he wanted to get back to work, and Alexi knew better than to sit and chin-wag with him. She was still irritated about the bug, however.

"I made contact with a possible today, but need to check it out. Follow up at the Trevi tomorrow." She finished the tea, listening for a response.

"Good. Keep us posted."

"I'm sending you digital photos taken today for comparison - can you get back to me pretty quick?"

"Sure."

"I'll wait."

Neil hung up the phone. She knew that he never said goodbye on principle, having heard once from someone that it meant you would never see that person again. Perhaps he had seen too much in his life, and too many people he had known were not seen again.

The man she had met at the restaurant near the Trevi fountain could be the Cougar. His advancing years would have changed him. But there was something about the shape of Cardini's face that just didn't look quite like the man she had met, and the recent photo was simply not clear enough to make a call.

She encrypted the pictures of the man and sent them to Neil for comparison. After making sure they were received, all she could do was wait until he replied. She left the computer on with the audio alert signal set so that she could get her response. It might take an hour, but it also could be less.

Computer - cell phone. Devices. Keeping it simple would be easier, some kind of all-in-one digital wonder. Maybe she would opt for something else.

She sat on the bed and leaned back with her feet on the floor. Needed to think about the man at the Trevi. Had his charm blinded her? She had felt something close to attraction, to be honest. Seldom met men her own age who were available, not going dotty, or a walking mass of medical problems. Not that he didn't fit the preliminary description. But he had managed to interest her in a way that was a bit disturbing.

And the Kling-on. Wasting precious time trying to shake the bastard. Neil had jeopardized things by trying out someone new on her – or was he testing her ability to pick up on surveillance? Who was he trying out? A wave of anger crashed through her again. Could she really trust Neil? Was she on her own here? No one had ever been inserted into her jobs before. Alexi groaned aloud. "Damn you, Neil!"

She went to the window, slammed it shut, and pulled the drape. She had a feeling there was another threat out there.

Chapter 10 - JR anger w/church

Jim Russell watched the Italian news channel, propped up at the head of the bed with pillows. The open window let in a bit of sun and air with sounds from the street below. Sounds of laughter came in and partially drowned out the television, so he got up and closed the window.

He went in the bathroom. Looked at his haggard face in the mirror, shrugged, gave himself a wry grin, and decided it didn't matter. Who was going to be looking at him, anyway? He needed to shave before he went anywhere, but there was time for that.

He got the bottle of Johnny Walker from his suitcase and poured himself a liberal amount in a bathroom glass. The pills were in his ditty bag on the back of the toilet, and he shook out two, tossed them back and washed them down with the booze. The warmth of the alcohol went down to his stomach and the numbing process began. Gradually, the pain would subside. Enough booze, enough Vicodin - and then oblivion. For the evening, hopefully for the night.

The pain was an old buddy that had gradually grown worse over the last year, and at first he learned to live with it. But there had been days when he wasn't able to think or respond quickly to situations, and finally he asked the doctor for pain meds. The booze was something new. Never been a drinker. Not in his line of work, where he had to be sharp. Always a sharp guy. Very sharp.

Now, he was focused on his one goal - to complete what he had set out to do - to bring it to conclusion. Only he could do it, of course, because he was the only one who understood it completely. The importance of it. He knew he was alone in seeing the true situation. He would have vindication for all of the things that had happened. The church. The priests. The hidden things he never shared....

He sat back down on the bed, put the drink on the night stand and painfully eased himself back to a sitting position against the headboard. He reached for the glass and saw that the tremor in his hand had grown worse. Would he be able to complete his project? He had to. It was everything he had worked toward for so many years. He was so close.

Chapter 11 - Gypsies

Alexi sipped her tea and watched the televised interviews of persons who would attend the upcoming ecumenical meeting of all the major religious world faiths at the Vatican. Although many were not at higher echelons of their governments or leaders of their religions, they had sufficient clout and decision-making power to bring some consensus to the agenda of the upcoming world ecumenical conference. Amazingly, some of the more radical elements were attending.

The talking head was an attractive, dark haired young woman who had a slight resemblance to Christiane Amanpour. She spoke in Italian, but Alexi could read the English subtitles at the bottom of the screen.

"Peace between radical elements of religious sects?" Alexi argued with the woman who couldn't hear her. "Yah, sure."

Alexi talked back at the screen. "Only the beginning of talks to follow - setting up the agenda for the big-ass conference." She took another swallow of tea. "Right. And everyone is gonna keep their promises. Yah, of course they will!" Alexi laughed out loud. Bull crap. It would be a miracle if even the first meeting was successful.

"Yah, let's have it all at the Vatican. Let's have a miracle!" Alexi slammed her cup down on the night stand. Intel already knew about the plan to sabotage the meeting and how it would happen. The Cougar – Stefan Cardini – and some kind of bomb.

That's why she was here. To stop him. But where was he now? If she could be followed and located, why wasn't Cardini located? Questions without answers piled up in her mind, and she flipped off the TV, got up and went to the window.

Alexi went over the plans for security in her mind. Her company had a contract to provide protection for the United States attendees. Other security firms were providing personal protection for other attendees. The Italian government and the local Vatican and Roma police were involved, as was Interpol. The Vatican was supposed to coordinate security so they wouldn't all be tripping over each other, causing more problems than they were hired to solve.

Who from Marsdon Security would be in Rome? The meeting was in three days. Her orders originally were to not make any contact with other company personnel. What the hell?

She had to eliminate Cardini before he caused incredible damage. Every hour was important. Too much time had already been wasted.

The alert on her computer rang. She accessed the message from Neil. There was an attachment.

Looks like you have identified a possible match. Be careful.
Neil

The attachment showed Cardini's face and the photo of the man in the restaurant both in frontal view, with points of comparison marked, primarily on bone structure. Most of the points compared exactly, but there were two that didn't match, at the nose and chin. Those were commonly reconfigured by plastic surgery. The man at the Trevi who called himself Joe Pelloni could be Stefan Cardini. He had used so many names over the years that no one was sure which one was the original.

She went to the window again. The sun was much lower, and she was hungry. Perhaps she would try out a new restaurant, someplace on the Piazza della Rotunda near the Pantheon. It was within walking distance of her hotel, and she felt like stretching her legs. She ran a brush through her hair, swiped on a bit of lipstick, and took a sweater.

Alexi remained alert to the possibility of being observed, but this time she didn't wear a wig, just her own black and gray hair. No blue contacts. She wore casual black slacks and the blue blouse, and looked like one of the innumerable American tourists of indeterminate age in Rome.

The cobblestone streets were busy with people going out for dinner at the various restaurants that offered a multitude of delights. She skirted the round Pantheon building with its deep fenced moat. The street had gradually been built up around it, and its original base was many feet below street level. Thousands of years old, it had been a temple for many gods - now it housed religious statues and relics honoring only a single God. Yup, can't have those pagan statues. She grunted in disgust. The Vatican could host a multi-religious conference, but couldn't tolerate differences in Rome.

Alexi crossed diagonally in front of the ancient building and headed for one of the restaurants, but was distracted by a small market with a display of cheeses and smoked meats. If she were simply a tourist, she would probably arrange to have some shipped. But on trips like this, she could not afford to leave any trace of herself by purchasing something and putting it on a credit card, or leaving a shipping order to her home. She looked in the window and assured herself that she could get the same things back in Ann Arbor.

A slight breeze blew across the piazza. She pulled out her sweater and draped it over her arm. She wanted to sit outside, but it might turn a bit cool. Some of the restaurants were already firing up the tall heating units that kept their outside diners comfortable. A number of people being seated. Alexi stopped at the second restaurant after looking over their menu.

"One person, madam?" he asked. She nodded, smiling.

The host led her to a table on the outside of the seating area.

"Hot tea, please." She decided it was a bit cool, stood up, put on her sweater, and placed her bag near her feet.

In seconds a small pot of tea and a cup and saucer was put down in front of her. She looked over the menu. Oh, wonder of wonders - the spinach tart. She sometimes made it at home and loved the pine nuts that dotted the top.

"Torta di Spinaci, please." She handed the waiter the menu, and he nodded his head and left. She barely had time to drink a sip of the tea when another waiter brought a small salad and a third waiter brought her a basket of crusty bread and butter and lit the candle in a red holder. One of the benefits of her job – travel and delicious food. For a little while, she could push aside the thought of why she was here.

As she ate, the light diminished and the voices of people around her made a pleasing murmur of sound. The fountain at the center of the piazza had its usual complement of young people, most of them incredibly thin by American standards. They sat and stood, talking and smoking cigarettes. Some stood next to their scooters. A couple left, the boy driving and the girl seated behind him, black leather-jacketed arms around his waist.

Alexi heard music and saw a couple walking past diners at the next restaurant. A woman in a long skirt shook a tambourine, and a man wearing a dark cap and black vest was playing a small accordion. Gypsies, the scourge of the cities of Europe. One of the restaurant waiters ran out, and spoke sharply to them. The man pulled out a small card and showed it to the waiter, who threw up his hands in disgust. The waiter rushed back into the restaurant and came over to Alexi's table.

"Watch your bag, madam. The gypsies, they steal everything!" He walked on to the next table, repeating in Italian what he had said to Alexi in English.

Alexi pulled her backpack onto her lap, smiling. She remembered the wonderful day with a gypsy family at the Agora in Athens and how no one had taken anything. In fact, just the opposite - they had offered to share their food with her. She had taken pictures of them and had bought a few small things from them, but nothing bad had happened. Someone to look down on in every culture. Here, it was the gypsies.

She listened to the songs they played, and ate her meal slowly. She understood gypsy culture and history, at least the parts she had read in books by contemporary Rom themselves. Hitler had tried to eliminate them, and thousands had died in the death camps. Yet here they were in Rome, playing and singing, passing a hat for the tips that were their due for livening up the dinner hour.

Why was she so concerned about the gypsies? Rooting for the underdog? Pity for people that experienced genocide? Perhaps she identified with them somehow – someone outside the mainstream.

When the gypsies approached her, Alexi pulled a few bills out of her bag, and placed them in the hat.

She smiled. "Grazi." The gypsy man smiled, showing a gold tooth in the front of his mouth. He nodded to her and looked her straight in the eye.

"You are very welcome." he said with a very American accent.

"Oh, are you American?" She laid down her fork and turned slightly to face him. The cap he was passing was a soft one with a stiff bill. He took out the money, shoved it in his pocket and put the cap back on his head.

"Dearborn - Detroit." His eyes were dark and turned up at the corners with his smile. Alexi estimated that he was in his fifties. His moustache and hair were black streaked with gray and his dark eyes twinkled in the candlelight from her table.

The gypsy woman standing with him wore a long skirt, a full dark blouse with long sleeves that had gold and silver thread that reflected, reflecting the gas lights around the restaurant. She was lovely, and her long, curly black hair was piled high on her head, held with a gold barrette.

"Ah, I am familiar with the area." Alexi had driven through the streets in Dearborn. Many Islamic people. She had heard that some of the gypsies were musicians who traveled back and forth between Chicago and Detroit, playing in nightclubs in both cities. "You go to Chicago, too?"

"Oh yes, ma'm." He pulled off his hat and moved on to the next table, the woman following him. Alexi went back to her dinner.

Amused that she had come all the way to Rome from Ann Arbor to listen to gypsy music by someone who lived that close to home. It truly was a small world.

She watched the pair as they collected their tips and walked away from the piazza past the Pantheon and disappeared from view. Something about them bothered her. Something different from the people she had met in Athens. She had sensed a wariness in the gypsies there - holding something back.

Yes. Like this pair had held nothing back. What you saw was what you got. Not quite right there. Were they pulling some kind of con? Well yes. She laughed at herself. Right. Gypsies pulling a con. She dug into her dinner and enjoyed every bite, pushing her paranoia down under the delicious food.

Chapter 12 - Meeting JR

It was early evening when Jim Russell walked across the piazza in front of the Pantheon and selected a restaurant for his dinner. He asked for a table next to one of the tall gas heaters, ordered a cup of coffee with orange liqueur and sipped it, grateful for the warmth.

An older woman with a black backpack slung over her shoulder walked along the same way he had come. She stopped to look in a store window and went to the restaurant next to the one where he was sitting. She looked at the menu posted outside the sidewalk seating. With all the young people around the fountain, motor scooters racing across the piazza, and the continual flow of tourists, she was the only older person walking alone. Not overweight as so many women her age were these days. Low shoes instead of ridiculous high heels. The slight sway of her hips was distinctly feminine. He might be on his last legs, but he wasn't dead yet. Not quite.

The woman appealed to him. Perhaps it was because she had done almost nothing to enhance her appearance. He was used to women in his age group with perfect hair styling and an abundance of makeup. He liked her face - the slight Asian look, and the way her hair flipped up on either side like tiny wings. She was wearing a rather plain pair of slacks with a loose blouse. She pulled a sweater from her bag and draped it over her arm before sitting down, gave the waiter her drink order, and then stood up again to put the sweater on. She looked like a competent businesswoman. Might be American.

He ordered his meal, asked for another coffee, and focused on thoughts about his research. The documents he was allowed to see in the outer rooms of the Vatican library had proven interesting but probably showed only a miniscule amount of the information he wanted. He knew that only a few people were ever allowed in the *sanctum sanctorum* of the most secured archival material. The area where he was working was more public, but still required special permission.

A pair of gypsies was standing near the fountain, playing an accordion and a tambourine. The song they played was 'Never On a Sunday' - one of the usual tunes played by both gypsies and the Peruvian flute players who came to the piazza.

A waiter at the next restaurant rushed out and checked to see if the gypsies had a permit from the city, and then rushed around warning his guests about the habits of the musicians. Jim had always heard complaints about gypsies stealing. He heard they were scamps, and you could never get a straight story out of any of them. He went back to eating a small plate of pasta with bits of chicken, and sat back enjoying the meal, ignoring a pain that took up residence in his back.

The gypsies stopped and sang another song near his table, and he pulled coins from his pocket and dropped them in the man's hat. The gypsy woman looked at him and lowered her eyes, pulling her head scarf more tightly around her neck. The attempt to be modest had the opposite effect and made him wish he were thirty years younger.

After paying his bill, he got up. Should he try to walk back to his hotel, or get a cab for the short distance? He felt weak, rested one hand on the table, waited for everything to stop spinning around him, and gained his balance. Damned medication. Not supposed to take it with booze. What did it matter? The feeling passed, and he straightened his shoulders. This was no way to live, doddering around, hoping he didn't collapse from exhaustion. It would be over soon.

Alexi saw an elderly man exit the adjacent restaurant and come her way. He walked carefully, as though somewhat unsure of his balance. His hair was white as Joe's, his face as lined, but patches of skin on his cheeks and forehead were reddened and shiny as though repaired with plastic surgery. The rest of his face was extremely pale, and his eyes were red-rimmed, with dark circles beneath.

Ah. He fit the description. Here, in the right place, at the right time. She needed to make contact immediately. He could be her target. The bone structure in his face was a close match to the pictures of a younger Cardini. She felt her heart speed up.

The man passed her, walking a bit unsteadily on the cobblestones of the piazza. No time to think about it. She'd lose him. She stood up, put money on the table, and grabbed her bag.

He was walking slowly, and paused as if to rest at the window of the gelato shop. Alexi approached the shop and brushed hard against him with her bag. He jerked away and grabbed the protruding windowsill to maintain his balance, giving her a scowl that distorted his face. The patches of red skin wrinkled and his brows pulled together over angry, dark eyes.

"Watch where you're going!" His voice was harsh and raspy.

"Oh, I'm sorry!" She turned to face him and saw his expression change from quick anger to disgusted irritation. "I'm so darned clumsy."

"At least you're honest." His mouth pulled sideways in a wry smile, but his eyes revealed nothing. She could see the hand at his side trembling slightly. "Not a common trait these days."

"I try to be. Honest, that is." A quick flash of pictures of herself in various disguises flicked through her mind, and she suppressed a smile. She put out a hand. "I'm Elaine Birdsall." He reacted automatically with a brief grasp and shake. She felt the trembling in his hand.

"Jim Russell. You sound like an American."

"I live in East Lansing, Michigan. You?"

"Did live in Chicago. Now I'm a New Yorker."

"Great place. Wonderful theaters." She had to keep him talking.

"If you like that sort of thing."

He was giving her the once over, and she restrained a shudder as his eyes traveled up and down her body. Play along, Alexi.

"Well, I did see a couple of shows there a few years back," she said.

"I like the jazz clubs myself." He didn't seem anxious to get away from her. Good. Now, who were some of the jazz musicians? She couldn't remember a single one. She had to delay him. Intel reported Cardini had been badly injured sometime in the past, with scarring reduced with plastic surgery. This man *had* to be her target.

"I'm going in for a dish of gelato. Perhaps you would join me? My treat, for being so rude." She gave him that special look, and saw his eyes drop to her breasts. Well, maybe the old guy wasn't in as bad a shape as he appeared. He seemed to be considering her offer.

"Oh, hell. Why not?" He reached out, opened the door, and followed her into the shop. Once she had purchased the gelato and they were seated at a small table next to the window, she waited for him to start the conversation. It was always wise to let other people think they were in control.

He asked her about herself and she gave him the Elaine story. He appeared to believe her, but there was no warmth like she had seen in the eyes of Joe Pelloni. The man's had a flatness that seemed to swallow everything and give nothing back.

"So what are you doing in Rome?" she asked.

"Research. I'm working on some material in the Vatican Library. Special permission." She wondered how he got through the inspection procedure. "I'm close to finishing an important project. My work will have quite an impact."

Impact? Yeah, a bomb would have impact, all right. She mentally shook herself and remembered her airhead persona. "Oh. On the Da Vinci Code?" She hoped her voice sounded just the right pitch to place her in the silly-female-following-every-fad category. "Wow! I read the book!"

"Not exactly." He straightened in his chair, and his hand holding the spoon trembled noticeably. The spoon slid from his fingers and fell to the floor. Alexi bent down, picked it up and dropped it in her bag.

"Woops! Can't reach it. Oh well." She waved over a waiter and asked him to bring another.

The man was definitely not in good shape. She wondered if she could manage to do him in before he simply dropped dead in front of her. Perhaps it would just be a matter of following him around and waiting to see where he would fall over without any help. Mentally shaking herself, she arranged her face into what she hoped was an interested expression.

"Oh my! In the Vatican Library? I'm very impressed! Have you found out anything interesting?"

"I provided the proper credentials. They bring out the material I request." He looked as though he might say more, but didn't.

"Well, good luck with your research. I might do some shopping tomorrow, but I really want to go through the Vatican museum, see the Coliseum, the typical tourist stuff. When you only have a few days...."

"I've already seen the sights," he said. "Used to come here to do research – on sabbatical – that sort of thing."

"Oh, were you a professor?" She listened carefully, taking mental notes as he told her about his academic, military, and subsequent work in the private sector. Some of the story fit Cardini.

"So what are you doing now?" She noticed that his eyes had now completely lost the previous guarded look. At this point, she could usually sense whether a target had established some level of trust with her.

"I was working on projects for my employer. Now I'm free to follow my own interests. Go where I please. No responsibilities." He looked as though he was quite pleased with that aspect of his life. Probably also used to making it quite clear to women that he liked it that way. Working his own project, sure. Something with impact.

"Me, too! I don't even have a cat!" She smiled.

"You said you have a family. Children, grandchildren. " For an instant she saw a slight twinge around his eyes and mouth. Could it be regret? Loneliness?

"But they don't live in *my* condo!" She laughed softly. "And I hate yard work."

"Same here. I'm living in an apartment, but I'll be moving soon."

"Where to?"

"I'm not sure." His voice was higher in pitch, more raspy. As though he caught himself telling her too much. "Well, I should be going." He put one hand on the table and pressed down to help himself stand.

"Yes, me too." She stood up and hung the strap of her backpack on her shoulder while moving her hand to the small camera on the strap, and took what she hoped would be his picture.

He cleared his throat. "If you like, I could show you the Palatine - if you aren't going to be too busy."

Surprised, she looked down at the floor for a moment as if considering. "Yes, I'd love that... but when?"

"I go there every morning just as it gets light. We could meet there." He turned his head away slightly as though expecting her to decline, waiting for a refusal.

"That would be great, Jim. I'd love it! Just give me a call. You got anything to write on?" Alexi slid her hand into her pocket, felt the small plastic card with the tracking dot, and slipped the dot onto her forefinger.

He took out his wallet and withdrew a business card, turned it over to the blank side and handed her a pen. She wrote down a secure number that would ring into her cell phone without giving away her location and made sure the tracking dot was securely fastened to the card. It was a movement she had practiced hundreds of times.

They set a time and place to meet. It didn't matter. She would know where he was as long as he kept his billfold with him.

He walked out, supporting himself slightly on the door frame as he exited. As she left, she went through the same doorway he had exited and stood there for a moment holding the door with her left hand while pressing a strip of tape on the portion of the doorway he had touched. She eased the tape into a partially opened envelope in her pocket. He had some agenda going, but what?

========================

It was completely dark when she came to her hotel. She was surprised to find the pair of gypsies standing just outside the door to the building.

"What do you want?" A clutch of fear gripped her gut, and she hoped that her training would be sufficient to protect herself. There appeared to be very few people on the street, and none within a safe distance of the pair that stood just to the left of the hotel door.

"It's okay. We need to speak." The woman was talking in a distinctly American accent. She carried a dark velvet bag and was still holding the tambourine that she had played while singing earlier.

"Neil sent us. Marsden Security." The man's words were a shock. She had never had anyone from the company approach her while she was on a job, and wondered if there was some problem, some reason she was being pulled off. Or were they really from Marsden?

"Is there some...?" She hesitated.

"Something about your cell phone - he couldn't get through. Can we talk inside?" The man motioned to the hotel lobby.

Remembering the young man at the hotel desk, she thought for a moment. Seeing the way the couple was dressed, she doubted if they would be allowed in the hotel.

"No." She motioned toward the alley. It was not always private, but with luck they might be able to talk for a moment.

They went into the alley, far enough not to be seen from the street. Alexi looked up at the rooftops and saw nothing but the clean lines of the buildings.

"Now - what?" She was nervous about meeting the strangers at this time, and again hoped that they were what they said they were, but now she doubted they were actually gypsies. Also, she wondered why Neil would be sending someone to make any contact with her whatsoever. The whole thing made her nervous.

"Neil found out that the man you are looking for is doing some historic research in the Vatican library or archives. Some special arrangement with the church. He's inside every day, and has contacts that can get him into other areas. The info just came in." The man shifted his accordion on his shoulder. He looked around, pulling his cap down farther over his face. "Sorry. He wanted you to know."

"I already know that."

"There's some concern about your safety. We can provide you with some back-up if you need it." The 'gypsy' woman spoke in a low voice.

"Are you really with the company? I need some proof." Alexi had never seen these people before, but she seldom went to the office and many employees had been hired but were spread out on various jobs.

"We came on just after you left, but we've been working over here - some in Eastern Europe," said the man.

"We have to leave now," the woman was looking at one end of the alley and then the other. So far it was still deserted. Alexi knew that would probably not last.

"Here." The woman held out a cell phone, and Alexi took it.

"Just punch in this number." The man gave her a small piece of paper which he took from inside his cap. "Ask for Sam or Donna."

Alexi put the paper and the cell phone in her pocket. "I doubt that I'll need..." She was extremely angry with Neil. First the 'Velcro' bit tailing her around the continent. Now this - two more people to contend with. She liked working alone. People were a problem. What did he think? That she couldn't do her job alone anymore? The gelato threatened to come back up into her throat and she swallowed strongly.

"Thank you. You'd better be going..." She turned to go back to the alley entrance, looked out and saw that there was no one within a block of her hotel on the street. One taxi went by, but it had no passengers. She turned to the 'gypsies' again, but they were gone. The alley behind her was empty.

Chapter 13 - Not another bug

Alexi checked her room for bugs with the hand-held device. It seemed to be just as she had left it before going to dinner. The back came off the new cell phone the fake gypsy gave her came off with some difficulty, but appeared free of extraneous devices. She made a black mark with a Sharpie on the base of the phone, and wrapped one of the rubber bands she kept in her cosmetic kit around it to make doubly sure it didn't get mistaken for the other one.

It was now close to ten o'clock, and she carried the desk chair over to the door, slid the back under the knob and halfway secured the legs in the carpet. It wouldn't keep anyone out, but it would at least make some noise if anyone tried to get in. She pulled back the drapes and checked the window locks again.

Paranoia? Precaution? She had her routines in hotel rooms. It didn't pay to get sloppy, but she needed some semblance of security while she took a bath. Alexi was still plenty angry with Neil and the company for interfering in a delicate operation. Hopefully, the so-called gypsies would be working protection for delegates to the meeting at the Vatican, would leave her alone, and let her get on with her job.

Alexi automatically checked the bathroom one more time. While the hot water ran, she examined the contents of a little wicker basket on the counter. A small bottle of shower gel was provided, and she dumped the contents in her bath water - just one of her little hotel tricks, a bit of spoiling herself away from home.

The turquoise gel plopped into the bubbling water, and she saw a dark object fall to the bottom of the tub. Without thinking, she reached in the steaming water, feeling immediate pain as her fingers and wrist turned bright red.

"Shit-shit-shit!" She turned on the cold water faucet at the sink and held her hand under it until the pain receded. Her hand was still red, but it didn't hurt quite as much.

Turning off the hot water in the tub, she reached over with her now-pink hand and turned on the cold water, letting it run until she could put her hand in the water without burning herself. The dark object that fell into the tub was - of course - another bug that she had missed in her survey of the room. Her hand-held bugging detector had missed it entirely.

After another burst of curses - this time in several languages - she dropped the device to the floor, pounded it with her hairbrush, and flushed it down the toilet. The bottle of lotion and other hotel toilet articles were dumped and checked for bugs.

"Damn you, Neil! I'm not going to miss my bath!" She spoke aloud. Now she was talking to herself. It was only a matter of time, and she'd be in the same shape as the bad boys she was hired to eliminate. Alzheimer's would set in, or some kind of senility, and she'd be ready for the glue factory.

She undressed, not choosing to look at her body in the mirror. She had full breasts, but they were beginning to sag. Although her belly was fairly flat for someone her age, and her muscles quite firm, she wasn't interested in surveying the damage.

Of course, her semi-burned hand was uncomfortable at first, but the pain receded. She lay back in the tub and let her body go limp, using the old technique of starting at her toes and working upward. The neck muscles were always the most difficult, but the hot water helped. Letting the tension gradually drift away, she finally relaxed.

The two cell phones sat on the desk in her room next to each other, and when one of them rang, she was already out of the tub drying on the big towel. Her regular cell phone was set to vibrate as well, and she felt the vibration as she picked it up.

"Yes?" She kept her voice neutral and low.

"Sorry about the gypsies." Neil had known she would be angry. "Tried to ring you, but your cell must have been off."

"No. It's been on all the time." The cell phone had been in her pocket when she went to dinner, and she would have felt it vibrate even if there was too much noise to hear it ring.

"Don't know, then. The call didn't go through. Maybe a satellite problem." He sounded sincere. She felt her anger diminishing.

"Perhaps."

"Well, hope the intel is useful."

"Thanks." She adjusted the towel and knew her wet hair was standing on end. She had dripped water across the floor, and felt chilly. "Is that all?"

"For now. Maybe something tomorrow. We're short on protection for the U.S. delegates."

"Neil! I can't be in two places at once!"

"In case you're done by the time they're due to go back." He hesitated.

"Not my job, Neil." She pulled the towel up and flung it over her head, trying to dry her hair and talk on the phone at the same time. "Also, while you're on the horn - I found your other bug in my room, in the shower gel."

"Oh. No."

"Not one of yours?" She managed to pull the towel off her head and let it drop to the floor, and stood watching goose bumps rise on her arm.

"No. Not ours, unless I'm missing something." His voice rose slightly in pitch, and she recognized signs of stress. "Oh, and that guy we had following you hasn't reported in yet."

"Oh." As far as she was concerned, the damn Kling-on could rot in Sorrento.

"What did you do with it? The bug?" He was concerned now.

"Flushed it."

"Oh." There would be no way to trace the source now.

"Sorry. Thought it was one of yours."

"Not ours."

"Well, that changes things. I'm outa here." She didn't need this.

"So you're moving?"

"Yup. Second time for crissake. And I think I might have found our target." She was already in the bathroom, packing up. It would be impossible to sleep in this room.

"Fantastic! Okay then. Give me a call when you can."

As she dressed and packed once again, she felt the anger with Neil receding and tiredness that was part age and part jet-lag set in. She wolfed down a thick piece of chocolate for energy to get to another hotel. Hopefully there were taxis patrolling nearby.

She wiped down her fingerprints. The washcloth and bath towel could contain DNA, so she ran hot water in the bathtub, added some grains of a compound from her toiletries bag, and dropped the towel and washcloth in. Any other bits of her in the tub would be destroyed.

Alexi clumped tiredly down the back service stairs to an outside entrance carrying her suitcase, wearing her backpack. The alley was semi-lighted and empty of occupants. The cats commented briefly but she declined any response.

As she went through the motions of setting herself up again in another hotel, she realized her hair was still damp. No matter.

After going through her security routine she muttered a mantra that consisted of "crap-crap-crap," "shit-shit-shit" and "caca-caca-caca." After several repetitions, she calmed enough to think about sleep. Alexi pulled on her night t-shirt and a pair of bed socks to keep her feet warm and crawled under the covers.

=======================

The young man who had followed her from Amsterdam entered the hotel room quietly. In the dim light from the closed window, he could just make out the shape under the duvet on the bed. He raised his gun with its long silencer and shot three times, walked over and pulled back the cover. Feathers from the duvet floated up.

A row of three pillows had been skillfully arranged. A dark wet washcloth lay on the pillow where her head should have been.

Chapter 14 - Cardini's cover

Stefan Cardini sat in the study room at the Vatican archives, his laptop in front of him next to a folder of yellowing documents. He wore the required white cotton gloves used in handling the 400-year old papers, careful not to contaminate them with anything but his breath. With forged credentials he had been given access to some of the lesser important documents. He had already determined his course of action and escape route.

In three days, the documents would no longer exist. Some had been copied and duplicates were in Paris and North America. Some had not. There would probably be furor over the loss of the archives. He shrugged.

Cardini didn't have any interest in the religious documents in the archives. His interests over the years had been in the things people invented in order to kill each other. His private collection of weapons housed in a London warehouse would be moved to an island in Indonesia once this last job was done. His home in Phoenix would be sold. His investments in the companies that manufactured war materials would provide a more than adequate income.

This was just a way to occupy himself before he destroyed the people threatening his livelihood. Simply spending a few hours on a minor project that had caught his interest over the years. The weapons created by North American Indians to fight with were indeed clever. The ignorant missionaries provided access to the materials the Indians used to make the very weapons that killed the European intruders. Amazing. He found the same occurrences in his studies of weapons in other parts of the world.

These rare documents had never been included in publications or on the Internet. They were not considered important - letters, receipts, invoices, and other financial records between the diocese and the missions in the New World. Just extraneous material which appeared to have nothing to do with the early missionaries' journals. He took a few notes. Might write about it sometime. More important, it gave him the perfect cover for access to the Vatican.

An early call assured him that the small nuclear suitcase bomb was being delivered tomorrow. The case would be heavy, but since the bomb was not large enough to take out the entire city of Rome, he could handle it. He trusted the people who obtained the uranium and created the device. They had collaborated for many years. He would be long gone from Rome before he used remote detonation.

Cardini went outside for a cigarette. He watched busses pull in and spill out tourists. A young black-uniformed Carabineri holding a lit cigarette came over and joined him in the shade of the building.

"It is very warm today," the policeman said in English.

"Many tourists," Cardini responded.

"Every day. Are you a tourist?"

"No. Researcher."

"American? Canadian?"

"American." Cardini wondered why the policeman had approached him. Probably just used it as an excuse to take a cigarette break. "It is much cooler in the archives."

The Carabineri's English had only a slight trace of an accent. "What is the subject of your research, if I may ask?"

"Old military and trading post records of early missions in North America." Cardini had only half-smoked his cigarette and wished the policeman would go away. Apparently not.

"Missions to the natives? Bringing the word of God to them? Are you religious?" The young policeman took another satisfactory drag.

"No, just interested in their inventiveness." Cardini was uncomfortable with a stranger asking questions. "The missions provided blacksmiths, and the Indians used scrap metal to make arrow points."

The Carabaneri grinned. "Clever savages."

Cardini returned the smile. "Tricky devils. When the Americans ran the telegraph across the continent, they even climbed up the poles and removed the glass insulators and made arrow points out of them."

He was warming to the topic with the man, had to be careful. He raised his foot, put out his cigarette on the bottom of his shoe and put the stub in his pocket. He never left traces of DNA, so there was nothing in any databank for a comparison. Saving the stub was done out of habit. "Well, I've got to get back to work."

Back in the archives, he put the white gloves on and continued leafing through letters in the gray cardboard archival box. Only a couple of hours before he had to leave. At one time, he had thought about writing a book. Now, he just wanted to get this job done. He was financially secure enough to retire to the island and the lovely young woman who was supposedly waiting for him.

He rotated his shoulders, and glanced at his watch. He planned to meet the woman he had talked with at the restaurant on the previous day. What name had she given him? Elaine something. Birdsall. Yes. Like the Londoners would say - a bit of a sexy bird. It would be a welcome distraction. The message he had received the night before alerted him to what she was up to, working surveillance for some American security firm. Thought she could get close. Sure. He always let them get close.

His work was interesting at times, but it meant keeping up his physical strength past the time most men would be able to maintain themselves. He ran every day, and occasionally went to a gym for a workout. He knew he was in far better shape than most older American men, but the years were beginning to creep up on him. Nothing lasted forever.

Cardini had left extended family and old friends behind years ago, never married, and once his parents and only sister died, he had no one that close. Women, of course, a parade of them had run through his life. Usually girlfriends that stayed for weeks or months at his huge house in Phoenix and then moved on. He had access to enough sex to satisfy him, and always an abundance of the best food and drink. It had been a good life - once he left the low paying agency job. But now, after this last job, it was time to retire. He could live well - this job would guarantee his income would continue.

He left the Vatican complex, walked across the busy street to a line of taxis waiting for fares, selected the first one, and got in. "The Trevi Fountain, please."

Traffic was heavy. Motorbikes and scooters were abundant, and small trucks and automobiles were everywhere.

Cardini watched a worker shoveling street debris into a hand-pulled cart, working carefully with a pair of Carabineri watching, their uniforms a reminder of the ever-present Italian government. In a few days there would be more than enough debris to keep the man busy.

Chapter 15 - Date with J.P.

Alexi wore the blonde wig and blue contacts she had on the day before. She sat in the restaurant - Elaine Birdsall from Michigan - a bio she had used before. The other personae were tucked safely in the top of her wig. She smiled smugly, thinking how there were several other people sitting on top of her head.

A few people were standing and sitting at the Trevi Fountain, and tourist groups explored the area. With her back to the racks of the tourist shop next door, she felt somewhat exposed, since someone could come up behind her. She liked to sit with her back to the wall, able to see in all directions. However, if she attracted more followers, she could easily slip into the tourist shop.

She took out her knitting and began working on the sock, using four double-pointed needles, watching a new black-and-white pattern emerge on top of the bright red stripe she had knitted previously. This patterned yarn was interesting.

When Joe Pelloni emerged from a taxi at the corner and began walking toward her, she watched him under lowered eyelids. He was slim, walked easily, and his white hair caught the sunlight. He came directly to her table and sat down.

"Hi. Elaine, right?" He smiled and she noticed that his teeth were well cared for, a bit yellowed with age, but apparently his own. My goodness, his own hair and teeth - not bad for an American. And no beer belly, either. She smiled back, putting her knitting on the table. Too bad he might be her target.

"Right. Joe Pelloni, right?"

"Absolutely!" He reached over and smoothed out the partially knit sock. "For anyone special?"

"Not really."

"I've never seen yarn like that. Is it something new?" He sat back in his chair, looking directly at her.

"It's been out for a while. Makes its own pattern. Quite fun to knit, really. You never know with a new skein just how it's going to turn out." She wrapped the loose yarn around the skein, skewered the whole thing together and slipped it in her bag.

"Have you ordered?"

"Not yet." The waiter came toward their table with menus.

He ordered the stuffed squid and risotto. She preferred the squid fried crisp with lemon drizzled over it, but also ordered the risotto flavored with saffron and parmesan cheese. They talked little while they ate, and they finished rather quickly.

"So. What are you doing in Rome?" she asked.

He looked at her, apparently evaluating how much he was going to say. She wondered if what came next would be a lie or the truth.

"Research. I'm working on some documents in the library at the Vatican." He wiped his mouth with his napkin and placed it on the table. She looked at his hand. The one he used to pull the trigger on a sniper rifle? Her target was using Vatican library work as a cover.

She felt a prickle at the base of her neck, and straightened her spine. Keeping her face completely relaxed was a skill born of practice, so she arranged her features in what she hoped was an expression of casual interest.

"Oh? What kind of research?"

"Documents. About missions in North America. Mostly financial records, letters from relatives, things like that. Fascinating stuff. I've wanted to get at this for years." The expression in his eyes told her this was a topic he was actually interested in.

"Oh! Is it difficult to work on? Written in English?" She had to remember she was Elaine Birdsall. Not Alexi.

"No, most of it requires translation, but I'm fairly good at that. Can't speak very well in other languages, but reading's been a hobby." He picked up his glass and took a sip of water.

"I'm afraid I'm not very good at languages myself," she said.

"What do you do? Or should I say what *did* you do? I mean, are you retired or...?" He waited for her to respond.

"I'm actually a retired secretary. For the past five years." She looked in his eyes, mentally comparing his face with that of Cardini, and caught herself thinking that he must have been handsome in his youth.

"Where do you live now? You said you're from Michigan." He looked directly at her, and something made her want to tell him the truth. She stopped the feeling, giving herself a mental shake.

"Lansing. Well, actually East Lansing. I bought a condo." She looked up at him with her Princess Diana look which she hoped was shy and rather fetching. This Elaine Birdsall thing was beginning to catch on.

"So tell me about your research, Joe." She took a piece of bread from the small basket, and broke it into small bits, eating as she listened to him describe the fascinating documents he had been reading over that morning. As he spoke, she felt somewhat less sure this man could be Cardini. But his description was so close to the photos she had seen - and the research in the Vatican. It was just too close to the information she had been provided to be a coincidence.

Yet there was something about him. Perhaps that was the secret of Cardini's success, drawing people in. He talked about his research and interest in the artifacts of the era he was studying.

"Do you want to share a dessert? I can't eat a whole one, but you get two *cannoli* with the order." He looked concerned about pleasing her.

The waiter brought two plates, and they ordered coffee. The *cannoli* was excellent, the filling a bit firm, and the pistachio nuts crisp. Alexi brushed the powdered sugar from her fingers. She couldn't keep eating like this.

She also needed a tight rein on her attraction to the man seated across from her. He took out his cell phone and checked the time.

"I would like to see you again, Elaine. But I have to get back to my research. Unless you would like to accompany me." He wiped his mouth and hands on the napkin and pushed his chair back from the table a bit. "Are you interested in old musty things? Myself excepted, of course." She found herself not wanting to cut the afternoon short. "Perhaps they would make an exception and let you in with me."

"Hmmm." She tipped her head to one side, thinking, and then grinned. "Okay. Why not?" This would be a way to follow through on Neil's information about a man using the Vatican archives. Perhaps Joe was Cardini - the Cougar - but maybe not.

They took a taxi to the Vatican, entered the Library area through a side door and a series of hallways, and ended up in a small reception area manned by a priest who looked as though he taught boxing or wrestling as a sideline. Joe asked if she could enter the archives with him and was told that it would be impossible. There needed to be a letter of introduction, guarantee from a university professor, a review of her credentials verifying that she was who she said she was, and copies of her university transcripts.

Pelloni tried to convince the gatekeeper that he needed her secretarial services in order to do his research, but his ploy didn't work.

He turned to her and shrugged. "Oh well, I tried." He smiled ruefully.

"That's all right. You meant well. I have other things to do, Joe. You do need to get back to your work."

He walked her to the outside door, and they stood together on the cobblestones of St. Peter's Square in the early afternoon sunshine. Groups of tourists followed their guides, and the sounds of several languages reached their ears. Vendors were going up to people trying to sell them souvenirs, and there were a few gypsies about as well. The women were dressed in long skirts and head scarves, with small children standing next to them holding up souvenirs to sell.

"I'm so sorry about this!" Joe had to raise his voice over the noise.

"Don't worry. I'll be just fine. Perhaps we can meet again. I haven't seen all of Rome yet, and I'm really anxious to spend some time just playing tourist."

When she asked if he had anything to write on, he took a small notebook out of his pocket and handed her a pen. Hopefully, it was something he kept with him. She gave him the secure cell number and slipped a tracker on the card. The device was nearly invisible, clear plastic holding a tiny microdot.

"How about dinner? I know a really interesting place. We could meet there - about eight?" He looked as if he really wanted to see her again.

"All right. Fine. Where is this place?" She smiled and adjusted her bag, wishing it were a bit less heavy.

He pulled out his cell phone and thumbed an ap. "It's on Via Monterone, near the Pantheon. It actually serves French food, but also other countries are sometimes represented. It's called *L'Eau Vive* - you'll love it! Do you want me to pick you up?" He looked at her, waiting for a response. No way would she let him know where she was staying.

"I think I can find it. Sounds interesting." She hoped her response sounded like the person she was supposed to be, an innocent traveler, happy to have his company.

"Fine! I'll see you there... eight o'clock... don't forget!"

She hadn't caught it when he used his cell phone to take her picture. Cardini slid his thumb across the images of St. Peter's Square, his exit routes, and came to the most recent photo. He had captured a good full front image. Needed to be sure.

Chapter 16 - J.P. himself

He looked in the mirror and turned his head, pulling back the hair that hid the scars from the last surgery. They were as white as his hair, and he mentally complimented the doctor on such a fine job. Perhaps that last time it hadn't been as important, but he knew it improved his looks.

He bent and touched his toes, bent again, and was relieved to hear nothing. No cracking in hips or knees. Although not everything worked as well, some things still did seem to function.

Cardini sat on the bed, swung his legs up, and leaned back against the pillows. He picked up the remote and found the news channel. Chose the French language. Always a perfectionist, he tried to listen to or use at least three languages every day for a few minutes. He repeated the words of the advertisements, practicing inflection and accent more out of habit than necessity.

He kicked off his shoes and let them drop over the edge of the bed. As he stretched his arms over his head, he felt a twinge in his abdomen, probably scar tissue from the bullet he had taken in Ireland. He concentrated on the news of the upcoming planning meeting at the Vatican.

The announcer was highlighting the plan for the ecumenical planning meeting. Only two days to go. Bullshit! People on the planet would never get along. They all needed what his partners had to sell - more ways to kill each other.

They made their respective fortunes on the continuing altercations between and within countries. Their trade in munitions, biochemicals and defoliants was ongoing and lucrative. The conference would interfere strongly with future income. But he would take care of that. After appropriate action, the conference would not take place - dropped as an impossible dream.

This would be his final *coup de grace.* The other jobs were minor compared to this. Just one minor nuclear explosion was all he wanted. It didn't have to be a huge one, but it would be the first use of a nuclear bomb in a real situation. There had been so many tests, and he was tired of it. He had seen to the transport of countless bombs and nuclear materials over the past years, but no one had been brave enough to use them. With religious leaders getting together to work out their differences, governments and economic leaders would follow. There was a real chance that the ongoing wars would diminish.

Of course, there was no chance that humans would ever really get along with each other. But with the economic incentives being discussed, many insurgencies would probably disappear. Men and boys employed at a decent wage would be less likely to go out in the streets and start throwing stones or blowing themselves up. All one had to do was look at the United States and its allies to see that

His plan would be easily carried out. He had access to the building, but the Pope appeared at regular times in St. Peter's Square, often with a huge audience. It would be a replay of other jobs, and he felt the old excitement at the thought of having one last chance to use his skills.

If course, there was always someone that wanted to stop him from carrying out his work. Thus far, he had been clever, and stayed one step ahead. He had made the necessary precautions, and never made close friends with anyone. It was too risky.

The woman - Elaine - seemed so naive and trusting. Perhaps too trusting. Perhaps not as naive as she seemed. Somehow, she didn't quite seem like an Elaine - and he wondered what she carried in that big bag of hers. It would be a shame to have her eliminated, but he couldn't take a chance.

He spent the next hour comparing the picture he had taken of Elaine with a database. It was amazing how much information he had obtained by simply capturing a photo.

Yes - interesting. His instincts were still functional. She was Alexandra Rostov, retired from a security company in Ann Arbor, Michigan. He recognized the company and knew what it did. Retired? Probably used to do protection – or maybe really a secretary. Now she was doing surveillance on contract. Clever woman. Hired to keep an eye on him, and got in close. He nearly fell for her airhead act, too. Obviously, at her age she was no threat, but he didn't need complications, and she would be in contact with others who were a bigger threat.

She was an impediment. And she was onto him. Too bad. Impediments were inconvenient but could be eliminated. He began punching numbers into his phone.

Chapter 17 - Checking out the old guys

Alexi caught a cab to her hotel, locked the door, swept for bugs, had a tea-and-pee, pulled out the things she needed from her bag - all routine - running on automatic.

She laid out the fingerprint tapes on a piece of dark paper and dusted them with powder from one of her small medicine bottles. A pair of extra strong reading glasses acted almost like surgeon's loupes. She put them on, looked at the sharper images, and found them usable.

The man who called himself Jim Russell had been careless about leaving fingerprints on the cup and doorway. She laid a thin sheet of plastic over the dusted prints and used a marker to find identification points. Another been there - done that - worked in the company lab for a few weeks once when she broke her ankle.

She turned on the laptop, and used company codes to bring up the analysis site, entered the markers, and it began running its search. It took longer than it looked on television forensic programs. Two tapes had the fingerprints of a James Russell from Chicago, Illinois. Retired historic researcher and private consultant. The photo of Jim Russell in the database showed a younger version of the same man, but with more scars. Before his plastic surgery. It matched.   The file on him came from a military source, and she read it carefully. Prior to entering the military, he had attended the University of Chicago. He was in a type of special forces unit in Korea, and for a short time in Viet Nam where he was wounded. After his tours of duty, each time employed as a private consultant doing historic research. Never married, no children. No family mentioned. He checked out, and yet there was something that was not quite right. It would have been a perfect cover for someone like the Cougar. Perhaps a little too perfect.

She got the flash drive from her knitting case and slipped it in the computer. The recent picture of Cardini came up. It should have been sharper. The picture of the man from 30 years ago was clear, but it could have been either of the men she had met in the past two days. Neil had said that Pelloni was her target, that he had a match using more sophisticated programming.

She went over the old fingerprint information on the Cougar, and found a different set of prints from those taken of Jim Russell. Alexi had read an article about fingerprint transplants and considered that possibility. The height, weight and present condition of the subject could be a match for either man. Perhaps the teeth. She looked in the file again. It was believed that the target had his own teeth with several bridges, but by that age, who didn't? Besides, she wasn't likely to be able to check out a guy's mouth that closely unless he was unconscious.

Identifying marks? Tattoos? The Cougar had none, and except for a mole on his upper arm which had been removed at one time, leaving what looked like an old smallpox vaccination scar, there was nothing. Many people her age had been vaccinated for smallpox, and although most of the scars had disappeared over the years, some still remained.

Well, she had dates with both men, tracking devices, and perhaps she could gather more data - the dinner with Joe near the Pantheon sounded intriguing. Meeting Jim on the Palatine Hill in the morning would mean a bit of a hike. She hoped he would be there and not pass out on the way.

Chapter 18 - Interesting date

Although her hotel was only a few blocks from the restaurant Joe selected, Alexi took a taxi rather than risk getting lost or being late. She wore the blonde wig and same contacts she had on at the Trevi Fountain.

During the short ride to the restaurant she realized that previously she had hoped Joe Pelloni wasn't Cardini. Now, it looked like Jim Russell wasn't her target, but there were ways of doctoring information in data banks, especially if he had access to that sort of thing. Russell seemed to be harboring a deep internal anger, something she didn't sense in Joe. But who knew? It might be that neither of them was her target, and she had been wasting her time, which would be a disaster. It had to be one of them. She checked the tracker for Joe. It looked like he was already at the restaurant.

The taxi pulled up at a building on a side street. The Via Monterone. The windows were lighted, and she saw a couple entering the restaurant. A simple sign - *L'Eau Vive.*

Alexi walked up the few steps, entered, and saw Joe Pelloni waiting for her. A woman dressed in a Scandinavian costume escorted them up the stairs to a large room full of tables and chairs. Dark green tablecloths covered the tables with small white tablecloths on top, and the glassware and table settings were plain. The waitresses were dressed in various national traditional clothing. The place was lit softly by wall sconces above simple paneling. Soft guitar music was playing.

"What is this place?" Alexi asked as Joe helped her with her jacket and pulled out her chair. She sat down, looking up at him appreciatively. "There is something different about it."

"It's run by Carmelite nuns from different countries. They wear their national costumes. The music you hear is being played by one of them. They will want us to sing with them at some point in the evening." He smiled, apparently delighted as he saw her eyes widen in surprise.

"Really? My goodness. I would have never dreamed there was such a place here!" A nun wearing a white blouse, embroidered vest and long skirt came over and filled their water glasses and asked if they wanted wine. Joe looked at Alexi inquiringly, and she asked him to order. She would go along with what he was having. It would prove a bit more interesting, and she didn't want to waste time. There was too much she wanted to know about him.

It was difficult staying with her Elaine persona, but she managed by listening with interest to his description of the documents he was reading at the Vatican Library. He seemed to be focusing on historic weapons, which come to think of it – did fit the Cardini profile.

However, the ambiance of the place, the delicious food that was served, and the soft guitar music - all melded together. She had to keep reminding herself to stay on point. She wasn't here to enjoy herself. Now what was he saying?

"When Americans ran the telegraph across the continent, the Indians even climbed up the poles and removed the glass insulators. They made arrow points out of them." He was eating a piece of bread and waving it around as he spoke. Alexi adjusted her shoulder bag strap on the back of the chair, and managed to aim the small camera in his direction. She caught him in mid-gesture, a full front facial image.

Now if she could just get his fingerprints. The knife he used to butter the bread probably had wonderful prints. It was one thing to get Jim Russell's. But stealing a table knife from a restaurant run by nuns? That would take some thought. Perhaps if she took the knife in the bathroom and used tape...

"Is the Vatican Library the only place where you have done your research?" She noticed that dishes were being removed from the table prior to dessert being served.

"No. There is a Jesuit order archive here in Rome, and another in St. Louis, Missouri in the states."

"Really! Have you been to the one in Missouri?" She eyed the knife and wondered how she would be able to remove it before the table settings were taken up by the nuns who were piling dishes in tubs and carting them off for washing.

"Yes. Plenty of material there, and also at the archive here in Rome. A lot of duplication, actually, but some documents are only here." He drank the last of his wine, and then looked around. "Do you see a bathroom sign anywhere?"

"I think it's just behind you." She gestured with her chin.

"Oh, thanks. I'll be right back." He got up, his chair nearly tipping over backward. He righted it with an embarrassed smile, and left quickly.

She took her napkin from her lap and laid it on the table over the knife, then brought the knife and napkin to her lap. She busied herself stacking the dishes as though helping clear the table. When a nun came to the table with a nearly full tub, Alexi saw that the knife would probably not be missed.

She took her shoulder bag off the back of her chair, put it on the floor next to her, and slipped the utensil into a side pocket. Keeping her hand in the bag, she took out a small mirror and lipstick and applied a bit - a typical thing an American woman might do while a man was away from the table.

Joe came back and sat down at the cleared table. "Oh, it must be time for the singing, and then dessert." Either he actually was having a good time with her, or extremely adept at acting.

The guitar music was louder now, amplified through speakers near the ceiling of the large room. Small pale green song sheets were being distributed around the room to the diners. Alexi looked at the words - *Ave de Lourdes* was to be sung in French. She didn't know about her accent, but she could probably limp along if everyone else sang louder.

Joe had a pleasing voice, and she joined in on the Canto antico… *"O Verine Maria, Regina del ciel: A Lourdes ritorna, Il popol fedel.... Ave, Ave, Ave Maria...."*

Everyone in the room was singing along with the clear voice of the nun playing the guitar. It reminded her of a movie she had seen years ago of a singing nun - and wondered if the tune in that movie was ever sung in this place. How strange. Singing a religious song with a man she might very well eliminate.

The evening ended with a chocolate torte with hazelnuts and mint sauce. Alexi finished hers rather quickly. Too good. Joe was taking his time and asked: "So, how do you like this place?"

"Like my grandson says - it's awesome!" Alexi wiped her mouth on the napkin, laid it on the table, and took one last sip of water.

"This has been really great, Elaine. I don't know when I've enjoyed an evening with someone so much!" He stood up and helped her with her jacket, his hands lingering a little bit too long on her shoulders. Alexi suppressed a shudder.

They walked down the narrow street together to a more highly lighted area where taxis could be found. The Pantheon loomed darkly across the piazza, and she realized she could probably walk to her hotel. But even though he had a tracker, she should find out where he was staying.

"Is your hotel near here?" she asked, hoping she sounded casual.

"Not far. We could have a nightcap in my room." He put his arm around her and looked down at her with a question in his eyes.

She felt herself stiffen and pull away. A reflex. Don't let him get too close. "Oh, thanks, but I need to get back. I promised my son I'd call him tonight."

"Some other time?" She kept an eye on his hand as he put it in his pocket and was relieved when he took out a card. "Here's my phone number, just give me a call."

"Yes, I might do that. Thanks for a really wonderful evening, Joe." She made herself reach up to his face and gently stroke his cheek. A goodnight kiss? No way. "I guess I need a taxi."

There was little traffic. A Vespa scooter roared by with a young couple whose laughter trailed behind them. Headlights came toward them with the small light on top that indicated it was available. He stepped out off the curb and signaled. It pulled over and she felt herself anxious to get away from him. Fear? Her gut said so. Always listen to your gut. The driver had the door open to the back seat and she tossed in her bag. Too abrupt?

"How about if I meet you tomorrow at the Trevi Fountain again? Let's say one o'clock?" She kept her voice light.

"Fine! See you then!" He waited at the curb as her taxi pulled away.

She asked the driver take a right turn and drop her off at the next corner. Alexi was able to stay close to the buildings and saw Joe dart into an alley just ahead.

=============================

Pelloni smiled to himself as he took a shortcut to his hotel. She had been clever enough to swipe his knife for fingerprints while he was in the bathroom. No problem. He remembered the old Polish proverb: 'When life throws a knife at you, there are two ways of catching it – by the blade or by the handle.' He was an old hand at catching knives and hadn't been cut yet.

Not the first time he had reeled in someone on surveillance. Too bad the woman was on the other team. She looked like a good lay - nice tight ass, a bit athletic for her age. Fun while it lasted.

Chapter 19 – More investigation

Alexi wrote the address of his hotel on her palm with a ballpoint pen. She was sure he hadn't seen her. A light came on in an upstairs third floor window just minutes after he entered. She texted the location to Neil on her encrypted phone.

==========================

The night clerk at her hotel looked up as she went past the desk. She took the elevator and had her room key ready, held between her fingers as a potential weapon. Like most of her life now, always ready for the unexpected.

It was early enough that she should be able to do some research on Joe Pelloni. She pulled the mini-camera out of the small silver brooch on the shoulder strap of her bag. Wearing thin latex gloves, she took the knife from the pocket of the bag and placed it on a clean piece of paper on the desk. Adjusting the lamp, she followed the usual procedure.

She found a Joe Pelloni from Indiana, according to the federal database. The fingerprints matched. He had a military file and had worked for the CIA in Europe. The government files were sparse, consisting primarily of hiring and discharge papers. There was an old photograph which was a close match for the man she had just left in the piazza. Recent activity was listed as an antique business.

Everything he told her matched. She downloaded the picture from the mini-cam, enlarged the photo from the Cardini file and compared points from her picture with the old one in the file. Could be a match.

Alexi saved the material on the small flash drive with the Jim Russell material. Both men had files. Both gave her a story that matched the files. Either both of them were authentic, or one was giving her a song-and-dance that somehow made it into the federal database. One of them could still be Cardini with files that had been re-structured at the federal level.

Alexi laid her two cell phones on the desk and opened the one without the rubber band. Neil should be in the office.

He answered on the first ring. It sounded like he was eating something. "Yo." Crunch, crunch, crunch. "Neil here."

"Roma here."

"What's up?"

"I sent you the Pelloni hotel info. Did you get it?"

"Yup. I relayed it to others on the team there. They'll provide surveillance on both men."

She outlined her problem briefly, used the flash drive to send him the photos and prints, as well as the codes for the trackers on both men.

"Get some rest, 'Lexi."

"How soon can you run this?" she asked. She looked at the clock, remembering she had to be on Palatine Hill in the early morning.

"Probably a while. I'll call leave a message on your cell, that all right with you?"

"Try to get right on it, hey. That meeting is coming up pretty quickly here." She hung up, remembering not to say good-bye. She had always thought of it as something possibly happening to Neil. This time she realized that it might be her.

Chapter 20 - On the Palatine with J.R.

The phone rang at 6 a.m. and Alexi groped for it, trying to remember where she was and why she had asked for a wake-up call. She hung up and burrowed into the pillow again. No. Got to get up. Meeting Jim Russell... Palatine Hill.....

She turned over and saw hair on the pillow next to her. Who? Her heart jumped in her chest and she sat straight up. Oh shit. Her damned wig! Must have come off when she finally collapsed. She was still in her clothes from last. night.

Alexi checked her cell. No message from Neil yet. She showered, pulled herself together and made it out of her room in twenty minutes. Not too shabby.

The breakfast room was empty and she was quick. She made a meat and cheese sandwich using the prosciutto and fontina, smeared a little bit of butter on the roll and smashed the whole thing together and wrapped it in a napkin. She put it in her bag along with a container of yogurt, a small can of apple juice, and a plastic spoon. If Jim would like breakfast, it was available.

She left the hotel and flagged down a taxi within seconds. The trip to the Palatine took a while, morning traffic a bit heavier than she expected. The Coliseum loomed up ahead and the taxi pulled into the *Piazza del Colosseo,* making its way through traffic to the marked entrance to the Palatine area.

Near the Arch of Constantine, she got out, paid the driver, hefted her shoulder bag, and began making her way up the stone walkway. There were no others walking up, and without the distraction of anything but the sounds of traffic below, she thought of the thousands of people who must have made their way over these same stones, who walked between these same trees that marched up the hill on either side. It was easy to get lost in the history of the ancient place.

It took her a good half hour to find the spot where Jim had told her he would be. The small garden was down a few steps behind the ruins of one of the ancient houses. The steps were a bit slippery with morning dew, and she walked carefully. He was sitting on a stone bench beneath an olive tree. The vegetation was thick, and looked as though it was only trimmed on occasion. A low wall of gray-and-white volcanic tufa behind his bench was covered with ivy.

He looked up as she approached, and smiled guardedly, his face shaded somewhat by the branches of the tree. "You found me!"

"Yes! You gave good directions." She sat down on the bench beside him, grateful to give her legs a rest. "Have you been here long?"

"Since sunrise. I watch it from another spot, and then come here." He brushed one hand through his white hair and looked at her. "I thought perhaps you weren't coming."

"Oh, I'm an early riser." She brought out the food from her hotel, placing each item between them on the bench. "You hungry? I already ate. Brought you some stuff in case you wanted breakfast."

He looked down at the food, took in a deep breath, and then looked away. "I suppose I should eat something. I forgot to have anything before I came up here." With the trembling hand he reached for the container of yogurt.

She unwrapped the sandwich and left it lying on the napkin. "If you don't want all of it, just eat what you want. I had one of these myself."

"Thank you." He ate slowly, seeming to savor the yogurt. "We're really not supposed to have picnics up here, but if we take all the containers and don't make a mess....." She made small talk and looked around. A small lizard sat motionless at the base of a tree. Several tiny birds perched above them, interested in the possibility of a handout.

"Don't feed the birds - that's a dead giveaway to the park police."

"Okay." She gathered the remains of his breakfast, wrapped them in the thick napkin, and put it in her bag.

"Have you seen the museum?" He stood up, pushing himself slightly with one hand. He was weaker than she had thought, and she wondered how he had made it up the hill.

As they approached the museum he told her the history of the place, answering questions where he could. She wished for a moment that she was just a tourist. Then the reason for her being here kicked in. Someone had been following her. This was a bad idea. There were too many places for someone to hide, where an attacker could approach, or where a sniper could be waiting. She was glad to get inside the museum, and carefully evaluated other people in the building.

They walked the cool museum halls. She suggested several times that they stop to rest and he acquiesced gratefully. At each stop, he talked about the history of Rome and the displays. She had little opportunity to ask him anything about himself, and played the part of Elaine Birdsall to the hilt. Since she had heard much of this before, she spent part of the time studying his face and gestures.

As they were going down the path to the street she finally was able to ask him more about himself. He was having some trouble breathing and said he would tell her more later.

They found a low wall near the entrance where he could sit and catch his breath, and she noticed the trembling in his hand was more pronounced. He had lost nearly all the color in his face, except for the places where the skin was smooth stood out, a pink contrast to the pallor. He bent over and put his head between his knees for a moment and then straightened up.

"Sorry. Just need a minute here..." he said.

"That's okay. Should we perhaps go someplace where we can sit and talk." She smiled, and he returned her gesture with a wry crooked smile of his own.

"Perhaps we should." He remained sitting, his breathing labored.

"I'll get a taxi. Just stay here." She went to the curb and flagged a cab. When she got back, Jim was standing, and made his way slowly to the vehicle.

He gave the driver directions to a restaurant on the Tiber. Outdoor tables and chairs sat under a large canopy that fluttered slightly in the breeze off the river. A few small boats were gliding past, and a ferry loaded with tourists made its way down the water.

"Are you feeling better?" she asked.

"Somewhat, thank you." He picked up his coffee cup with both hands. He looked down at it the tremor in his hand ruefully. "Excuse this. Just started recently."

"No problem." She sipped her tea.

Alexi wondered if she should raise the subject of the upcoming meeting at the Vatican. She chanced it. "I was watching CNN this morning. My goodness. I didn't know you could get that on TV over here!"

"Oh, yes. They have everything. Even old movies. Have you ever seen the ones with Italian subtitles? Or the ones in Italian with English subtitles for the hotel guests?" He grinned. "I saw Mae West in *She Done Him Wrong* the other night. In Italian. Very funny!"

"I saw that back in the states! Great movie!"

"My favorite is *La Strada.* The music..." He took another drink of his coffee.

"Mine, too!" Okay, enough chit-chat. She hoped to lure him back to the subject of the Vatican meeting.

Try again. "The stuff about that meeting at the Vatican - to set up an agenda for future meetings of the different religious factions. That seems strange - to have a meeting to plan more meetings!"

"Yes." He was abrupt, and set his cup back down on the saucer a bit too hard. Did the subject anger him?

"Do you think they will be able to accomplish anything?"

"I doubt it. People are always going to fight each other. It's the nature of humans." His voice was a bit harsh now, and his face twisted a bit. "Man is only an animal, and like other animals, he will act with violence. There is no remedy for it."

"Is it just the men? I often thought that perhaps if women were running things...."

He stiffened. "Have you ever visited a woman's prison? You would revise your thinking. They are no different than men. And sometimes even more cruel."

"I hadn't thought of that. I was even surprised when I saw that some of the Italian police are women. Guess I just haven't kept up with things very well." She reached for the small teapot to pour another cup.

"I love the Swiss Guard outfits. Everyone takes pictures of them." She worked for the Elaine Birdsall persona hard this time, hoping that she sounded ditsy. She tried bringing the subject back to the Vatican meeting. "I wonder where that planning group will be meeting."

"Oh, they will have some private place, well-guarded, of course." He motioned for the waiter to bring him another cup of coffee.

"I suppose."

He seemed to be watching her with some thought on his mind. Perhaps he was onto her ruse. He might be one of those who kept their enemies close. Warning herself to be more careful, she eased into her chair again keeping her bag close to her feet.

They sat quietly for a few minutes, watching the boat traffic. A street vendor with puppets hanging from strings attached to a handful of wooden slats came to their table. Jim motioned the vendor away impatiently, a disgusted look on his face. Alexi wondered how Joe Pelloni would have handled the same situation. This man seemed to have an underlying well of anger that sometimes bubbled to the surface. It was in the dark flat lack of expression in his eyes, and a sense of some deep sadness that permeated his whole demeanor. There are many causes for that kind of anger and sadness, and she wondered about his past.

Breaking the silence, she asked "Where are you staying, here in Rome?"

He turned his head quickly and looked at her with a penetrating expression. "A small hotel. Not far from here. It's reasonable, and the food is good."

"Oh. I've been quite happy with the food in Rome. In fact, I think I'll have to go on a diet when I get back home!" She played the Elaine persona hard. "There is so much food in the breakfast room that I've been able to fix myself lunches."

"Or bring a poor man some breakfast." His eyes softened somewhat when he looked at her this time, and she saw a hint of something gentle, but only for a moment. Then he pulled himself back and sat up straight. He looked out over the river, and she wondered what he was thinking.

"I don't normally spend time with someone like you. My experiences with women have been..." He stopped, toyed with his cup and looked away from her. "Not so good."

"Oh. Am I that different?"

The illness now showed in the deep lines and pallor. "Yes. Very different."

She picked up her cup as though hiding embarrassment. "Is that a compliment?"

"Yes." He spoke quietly, and looked away again. "But it's too late for me to develop any long-term friendships."

"Too late?"

"Soon it will all be over. So nothing really matters now." He looked directly at her, and the pain that he had been shielding was apparent.

"I am truly sorry. Some illness? Cancer?" He did look ill. But she regretted the words as soon as they were out of her mouth. She had allowed a well of pity to open.

"In a way. Leukemia. No cure." He shrugged his shoulders. "So I'm here, finishing up a project. Not much time."

"Jim! I am truly sorry." She wasn't lying. The sadness in her chest felt like a heavy weight. At the same time in the back of her mind - a reminder of what his project could be, especially if he had nothing left to lose. Neil could have had the wrong information about this man.

"Being here with you, in a beautiful place. It is more than I had hoped for." He smiled again, the wrinkles and smoothened places in his face combining into a strange visage indeed. She realized that he probably maintained a straight face much of the time just to avoid appearing ugly. What he had just shared with her could put a different light on her evaluation of the man. Perhaps this was the underlying sadness she had sensed. But there was more, something to cause the anger she kept sensing.

"Thank you," she said, waiting for him to speak again.

"You know that place where we met - on the Palatine?" He leaned forward, and she knew this must be something important he wanted to say. "That is the place where I want to die."

Alexi took a deep breath and answered carefully. "I understand. It is lovely."

"But look what a trouble that would cause everyone. Having to cart my old bones down that big hill! The authorities would be furious!" He laughed again, the harsh retort a contrast to his quiet words.

"I'm sure they could manage. You wouldn't be the first person to die up there. That hill is a killer!" They both laughed, and she forced down her feeling of compassion.

Then he spoke seriously. "Back home, I thought of suicide. Coming here to do it. So I am here, with two last things to do." He looked out over the river again, and she followed his gaze, seeing another large ferry down below on the water, filled with tourists. Music from the boat floated up to them, and balloons bobbed from the roof of the vessel.

The incongruity of the situation crossed her mind. Happy tourists. Music and balloons. Talk of death and suicide. What had he just said?

"What is so important?" she asked.

He was silent for a moment and then began speaking. "I was in a bad accident some time ago. The insurance payment was substantial, and I invested quite wisely. I seem to have accumulated a great deal of money, and now I have no one to leave it to - no one that would use it wisely. I have to make final arrangements. Also, the draft of the book I have completed must be sent to the publisher. The information in it is extremely sensitive and valuable." He straightened up his back as though firming his resolve, and looked at her again, the flatness back in his eyes.

"So you are a writer - a researcher! Oh my, I don't know a thing about that sort of thing!" She was playing the ditsy retired secretary bit to the hilt now. "I have a friend that collects old cookbooks, but that's the extent of my reading, unless you count romance novels!"

"Yes, yes. My research will be published, but my findings are complex... so many religious factions." He seemed agitated now, and he brought the trembling hand to the tabletop in a fist, working it back and forth across the white cloth.

"Factions. Like the people coming here to plan that big meeting."

"Yes, like them." He warmed to the topic. "They think they know, and that they can fix everything. But they don't know. It is useless. There will always be wars. Always be one group angry with another group! So many people have died – for nothing! Good people. Islamic and Christian and Jew!" His voice rose in pitch and volume. A couple at the next table glanced over at them, and Alexi knew they had overheard his words. She hoped they didn't understand English. She never wanted to stand out in a social situation.

"And you don't think putting women in charge would help matters...." she smiled and tried to calm his obvious agitation.

"No! People are people. Most of them are stupid or evil. The ones in charge make promises they can never keep. The church people – the things they have done – the things they have got away with for years..." He stopped, and then turned his head away again.

"Not everyone is evil, Jim." Alexi spoke quietly. "Not everyone."

"Perhaps. Not you, perhaps." He looked at her and his eyes softened a bit. His hand was still trembling in its fist on the table, and he pulled it down into his lap.

"I'm not so smart, Jim. Maybe not completely stupid. And I don't think I'm evil. But I'm not perfect, either. Nobody is. We just all keep trying." She looked down, not wanting to meet his eyes. A dumb thing to say, considering what her job was, here in Rome.

He continued: "But what good does it do to try? Look around you! The history of this place is full of violence. The church... the church... even there you see the corruption. The greed is incredible. And all the priests that molested the young..." He stopped. "Are you Catholic?" The question shot out of him like a bullet.

"No. Are you?"

"No." He leaned back in his chair and let his arms drop to his sides. "Well, that was quite an outburst. You're a good listener."

"I've been told that." She smiled.

"I want to see you again. But I don't even know how to get in touch with you. Where you are staying? A telephone number?" He looked at her again, and the flatness in his eyes was back. A chill suddenly made her remember that she never let anyone know where she was staying.

She gave him the number that would ring on her cell phone, one especially used for circumstances like this. He wrote the number in a small book he took from an inside pocket. He gripped the pen tightly, and the tremor gave the numbers varying shapes.

"Just call me," she said. "Do you have a cell phone? Can I call you?"

Alexi put his number in her phone. "I'd like to see you again, too, Jim." She stood up, and put the strap of her bag over her shoulder. "Maybe tomorrow. I'm going back home in a few days."

"I will be busy today. Dinner tonight?"

She still didn't know what kind of research he was doing. Was that the one important thing he had to do? Or was it something else? He had been pretty evasive about it. "I heard of a good Sicilian restaurant called "The Mask" - do you like that kind of food?"

He stood up, pushing himself with his good hand. "Just give me directions and a time."

She pulled a guidebook from her bag, found the address of the restaurant, and he wrote it in his little book. They settled on a time, and she reached out to touch him on his arm. "I'll meet you there. This has been very interesting, Jim. Thank you for the tour of the Palatine. I'll never forget it!"

They took separate taxis, and she waved to him as she got in the vehicle. His face was serious, and he gave a half wave back.

Alexi now felt less sure that Jim was not the one she must take out. She was getting too soft in her old age. Compassion was never her strong suit and couldn't be if she continued to work for Marsden. Spending more time with the sick old man was cutting into her focus, but she still wasn't sure what that last thing was that he had to do. Maybe not sending the manuscript. Setting off a bomb was a last thing, pretty final, and what did he have to lose?

Chapter 21 - The mime threat

Alexi made it to the Trevi in time to see Joe walking across the piazza toward the restaurant. She paid the taxi driver quickly and got out, cursing herself for wearing the itchy blonde wig, and having to schlep such a big bag of stuff around Rome. At least she had opted for comfortable shoes and slacks.

Just as she was almost within a distance that it was possible for Joe to hear her, she saw the same group of Red Hat ladies coming around the corner of a store, a chattering, laughing group that reminded her again of a flock of birds. Good grief. She told them she was Judy Mayhew and hoped none of them would spot her and come over to chat. Or maybe she should tell Joe that she had used that as a way to get a ride on their bus. Perhaps she could avoid them, if she made it to the restaurant quickly.

She walked behind Pelloni across the piazza, trying to hurry to catch up with him. When she was a few feet from him, breathing a bit hard, he turned around. His eyes and mouth turned up in a big smile and she stopped her rush.

"Hey!"

"Well, here I am. And here you are." That had to be a good imitation of an Elaine Birdsall ditsy babe.

"Shall we get a table?" Joe took her by the elbow and led the way to the same restaurant, as the day before. Elaine took the same seat with the racks of the souvenir store behind her, the same seat.

"So how are the socks coming along?"

"I haven't even worked on them! This morning I went up on the Palatine!" She knew her wig was probably a mess, her makeup nearly gone, and her face flushed. "It was truly awesome!"

"I haven't been up there in years," he said. "Used to be one of my favorite places, but it kind of got old after a while. You know, been there, done that." He picked up the menu but didn't look at it, keeping his eyes on her.

"Yah - got the t-shirt, planned the execution....." She realized that the terms she had chosen were too appropriate, considering the situation.

Joe laughed. "I hadn't heard that one!"

A waiter came and asked for their drink order, and she decided Elaine would be a bit daring. "I'll have a glass of wine - something sweet."

Joe ordered coffee. They talked about the city and its people. The waiter refilled her glass and she began to feel a bit too relaxed.

The Red Hat ladies were making their rounds of the piazza, and settled in at a restaurant next to the one where Alexi and Joe were sitting. The leader of the group looked over and saw Alexi, but only winked and waved. Evidently she knew how difficult it was for an older woman to meet a good-looking man in a strange city. Alexi grinned and waved back at her.

Alexi was still not sure she might be tailed. There had been too many instances on this trip of Kling-ons and she had the feeling that someone was watching her. She felt the familiar chill on the back of her neck.

"Excuse me, Joe. I'll be right back." Alexi picked up her bag as she stood, and went toward the now familiar bathroom. She stopped to adjust her bag on her shoulder, turning slightly so that she could get a better look at the area behind the place where she had been sitting.

A mime stood to the right of the Trevi Fountain dressed in black and white jester's clothing, juggling a trio of white balls. Several yards away another person stood on a box, wrapped entirely in gold cloth wearing a King Tut headdress. A small box in front of the person was placed there for money. A small girl was standing in front of the ersatz mummy.

Alexi made her trip to the bathroom quickly, rearranged her wig and added a touch of makeup. She walked back to the table and saw the little girl drop money in the box. The figure bent over as if thanking the child.

The mime and the mummy must have been what she had sensed behind her, as she hadn't been able to see them from where she was seated. Was this some kind of setup? Joe had taken her elbow rather firmly and steered her to her seat.

He was just finishing a piece of mortadella. He popped an olive in his mouth and smiled as she approached the table.

"I just noticed the entertainment out there! Do you mind if I change my chair?"

"Of course not - come sit closer to me!" Joe pulled her chair around so that she was sitting on his right and could see the piazza directly in front of her. The opening to the souvenir store was on her right, and she felt comfortable again. The sense of someone behind her or watching her was gone.

She ordered tea and Joe's coffee was refilled.

"Dessert? They have tiramisu!"

"I couldn't hold one more bite! But if you..." She felt like getting away from him, but needed to maintain contact.

"I need to get back to my research, but a few more minutes with you would be good."

He leaned back in his chair and looked over at the Trevi and the mime, who was now juggling some small things, tossing them up in the air and catching them.

She didn't move when he reached over and put his hand over hers, holding it for a moment, not saying anything. She looked at him and they didn't speak, but she saw something else in his eyes. There was a hardening, something other than affection.

She pulled her hand back slowly, but again felt a slight chill on the back of her neck and down her spine. She hoped her eyes reflected the warmth of Elaine Birdsall and not the feeling of trepidation of Alexi Sinclair.

He turned his head slightly. His profile was recorded in her mind, with the sunlight on the Trevi in the background. The mime was still juggling, and the golden mummy was standing perfectly rigid on its box in the piazza. She knew that this was another image that would be stored in her memory.

"Tell me more about yourself, Joe."

He began by telling her about his life as a young man in a small town in the Midwest, playing ball with other neighbor kids, going to school. Joined the army, stayed in for several years, traveled to different places. His story partially matched the information she had been given. How he met a wealthy man that needed a bodyguard who was willing to tolerate Joe's absences while he attended classes at a university, and eventually hired him to work on various projects pertaining to his investments. It often meant researching documents investigating chain of possession of antiques and other historic objects.

"I found that I was pretty good at doing historic research. It kind of grabbed me on an intellectual level." He smiled, toying with his table knife. Alexi noticed how he handled the knife, flipping it over and over in a way that showed a more than a casual familiarity.

She leaned forward slightly, encouraging him to keep talking. "So are you done with the Vatican material yet? Ready to go to that other library yet?"

"Not quite, a few more days, perhaps." He laid the knife carefully on the tablecloth and pulled his hand back, as though he realized he had exposed more of himself than he intended. "I'm almost through with the journals and letters."

"It must be really time-consuming. So many hours searching for just one little piece of information?" She started playing with the breadcrumbs on the tablecloth, making little circles in them.

"It isn't like that, Elaine. I find so much that I just can't absorb it all, or have time to copy it, either! Especially when I have other things that need to be done." He stopped himself, and picked up the knife again, turning to look out toward the Trevi. "Hey - look at the mime! Is that wild or what?" As he turned the knife, it caught the sunlight. The mime glanced their way. A signal?

The mime was now standing on his hands walking along the cobblestones of the piazza toward their restaurant. He mime flipped up onto his feet, and pranced to the group of Red Hat women sitting at the tables at the next restaurant. Pulling a small black cap out of his shirt, he held it out and smiled as the women put money into it. A pile of euros nearly filled the cap, and he wadded them up and pushed them into a pocket of his baggy pants. Several patrons put money in the hat, and again he took it out and shoved it into his pocket.

As the mime came toward Alexi and Joe, she noticed a Red Hat lady wearing a velvety tan jogging outfit - the one with the powder-horn purse - leave her group and walk quickly toward the souvenir store. Alexi lost sight of her as she walked past the kiosks near the shop entrance.

The mime had emptied his cap, and held it out to Alexi and Joe. His face had lost its smile, however, and Alexi's saw him looking directly at her. His makeup was thick white and black and hid his true features. Joe dropped money into the cap and the mime shoved the bills into his pocket, replacing his cap with his other hand. When he took his hand out of his pocket she saw a small black gun with a silencer pointed directly at her.

She dove under the table and heard a single pop. All she could see were Joe's legs, and the mime's baggy pants and jester's shoes.

"Hey - watch out!" Joe cried out. She saw his feet pushing his chair back, heard a loud cracking sound and rapid excited talking around them in several languages. People were running away from the area.

As she came up from under the table, she saw the Red Hat lady standing over the now prone body of the mime, holding her powder-horn purse like a club. She was smiling broadly and her red hat was on the cobblestones. The gun was lying next to the mime's hand.

"Got him!" She turned to Alexi and smiled. "Nasty fellow, that." The mime was out cold.

The waiter and other had gathered at the back of the outside seating area near the restaurant door, and Alexi could hear the whine of a police vehicle. Joe stood as though in a trance, not saying anything. He suddenly straightened himself and reached out a hand to help her to her feet.

"Elaine! Are you all right?"

"I think so. What on earth?" Alexi saw the muscles in his jaw tighten. His mouth was a firm line. One of the restaurant waiters came over but Joe waved him off. Another waiter had a phone to his ear, evidently calling the police.

"Probably just some crazy person. The cops will take care of him."

"Well, I certainly hope so!" she said, keeping her Elaine intact.

"I've really got to get out of here, this will probably take hours! They'll ask all kinds of questions, and I'll simply never get my research done. I'm sorry, Elaine. I really have to leave! How about meeting at the Pantheon tomorrow, same time?"

"Okay." Alexi looked at him, at the mime lying in front of her, and at the Red Hat lady who was still standing there. Joe put some euros on the table and walked away rapidly, keeping to the edge of the piazza.

"Oh my God! I don't have any idea why that man would want to shoot me! But thank you so very, very much!" She reached out her hand and the other woman took it and pulled her into a soft, warm hug. She was considerably shorter than Alexi, which meant that the hug placed her graying hair at a level with Alexi's chest. Alexi felt as though she were hugging her grandmother.

"No problem, honey. Just glad I was close by and could help out."

"I suppose we have to stick around for the cops." By this time, Alexi wished she could have gone with Joe, but she would have to stick to the Elaine Birdsall persona. It was the only identification she had available.

"I suppose so," sighed the other woman. "Just hope they don't arrest me for assault!"

"With a deadly weapon?" Alexi giggled. She thought of her knitting needles. Perhaps she should start carrying a powder-horn as well.

"By the way, my name is Elli - what's yours? I forgot it. You said it on the bus."

"Elaine. Elaine Birdsall. "She didn't want to look Elli in the eye and tell an outright lie, and hoped that her Judy Mayhew persona hadn't been picked up.

"Right." Elli looked away, and then down at the man lying on the ground. Something in her voice told Alexi that Elli wasn't buying the Elaine bit.

The police had not yet reached the piazza. Elli bent down and picked up the man's gun and shoved it in her pocket, got her red hat and grabbed Alexi by the arm. "Let's blow this joint, before the cops get here, okay?"

"Yes!" Alexi grabbed her bag, and they marched off in the opposite direction from the way Joe had gone. No one at the restaurant attempted to stop them. Alexi looked back for a second and saw the mime begin to sit up, his hand on the back of his head. Turning a corner into a side street, they just got out of sight before the police car pulled into the piazza.

"My car is just over here." They walked quickly down the left side of the street and Elli guided her into a short alley where a small grey Audi was parked. Elli unlocked the door they got in.

"What about the bus? I thought you guys were riding on the tour bus?" Alexi looked over at Elli, waiting for a response, but there was none.

"How about I drop you off at your hotel?" Elli backed out of the alley, shifted the gears, and drove carefully down the street.

Alexi wondered where this woman had come from, and why she was helping but knew enough not to ask questions. Perhaps another tail from the office? At this moment, she could care less.

"It's near the next corner. Just let me off there." Alexi wanted to get away from this woman as quickly as she could. One more person compromising her job was just too much.

Elli didn't say anything, simply pulled over to the curb and smiled at Alexi as she got out of the car. She reached into her pocket, pulled out the mime's pistol, and inspected it for a second. She handed the gun to Alexi.

"Later on, there will be ammo at the desk at your hotel; look in the bottom of the flower vase."

Alexi's hotel was nowhere near the corner where she got out of the car. After Ell drove off and turned a corner, she hailed a taxi and gave directions to the hotel. The ruse about the place where she had been dropped off obviously had not worked. Then she laughed at herself. If the Powder Horn lady was sending shells for the gun to her hotel, she knew its location.

Chapter 22 - Asking Chaz a favor

After checking her room, Alexi fixed herself a cup of Earl Grey tea with hot tap water, kicked off her shoes, piled the pillows on the bed so that she could sit up and lean back comfortably, and punched in the numbers on her cell phone.

"Neil here."

"Roma here."

"Yo."

For the next few minutes she gave him an earful of her experience at the piazza, frustration with the way the job was going, and a description of the woman that had saved her life.

"Powder horn, huh?" He was eating something.

"Yeah. Powder horn. A big one."

"Not bad."

"Actually." She sipped her tea. "Think I'll get one."

"We could retrofit it." He crunched again.

"I suppose so." She sipped again.

"Well, you're okay, though?"

"For now."

"Any better fix on the target?" Crunching.

"I'm not so sure now. How reliable is the info from the feds?" Sipping.

"Probably not very."

"Thought so."

Silence. Crunching. Sipping.

"Well, Neil." Alexi put the now empty cup on the night stand. "I really like to work alone."

"I know." He sighed. "I know."

"This has never happened before. None of it. Kling-ons. Gypsies. Mimes with guns. Red Hat ladies. I'm stressed, Neil."

"Don't blame you. Want out?"

"No." She hated to be a quitter. Taking out another bad guy was definitely something she wanted to get a sense of closure on. But what was it with the mime thing? Who knew what her job was in Rome, and who would want to stop her?

"Oh, the woman with the powder horn? She gave me the mime's gun and said ammo would be left at my hotel for me."

"Umm. It's coming." Crunching.

"You knew about that? She's with us?"

"Uh huh."

"Crap, Neil! Don't you guys trust me? I can do this job without so much help - so please get people away from me. Please!"

"Not the mime, 'Lexi. We didn't do that. So watch your back."

Alexi didn't speak.

"So thanks. For the backup."

"You're welcome, babe." He hung up.

The GPS tracking ap on her secure phone showed the location of both men. Jim was probably at his hotel. His tracker wasn't moving. Pelloni was nearby and moving, then stopping and moving again. Meeting someone? Planning her execution? A chill ran down her back and she shrugged it off.

She checked the time - she wouldn't be meeting Jim at the restaurant for another few hours. Enough time to do another bit of research. She had a few ideas of her own.

Needed a very good hacker. Now. The best one she knew lived in Ann Arbor in her own house. Reliable and discreet, Chaz lived on scholarship money, and always needed more. She was amazed that he would finish a master's degree at age nineteen. He would probably graduate before he was of legal age to order a beer. Either he refused to face hacker realities, or just didn't care. Even though he was some kind of genius, at his age, everyone was invincible.

"Chaz?"

"Speaking." His conversations were usually brief.

"Need a favor, kid." She hated to put him in a precarious position, but this was an emergency. Chaz knew how to deal with encrypted files, and a whiz working with coded data.

She described both Jim Russell and Joe Pelloni, gave him instructions as to which government files she needed.

"I'm sending the stuff to you now. There's got to be something fishy about it. Maybe the files have been doctored for some reason."

"No prob. Just gotta finish one thing here. I'll get right on it." She knew he was probably carrying at least 18 to 20 hours of classes at the university, but still had time to play computer games with a group of international players in an ongoing competition. The computer equipment in his apartment took up more space than his meager accumulation of furniture and personal items.

Chaz was the only non-company person that she talked with about her contracts. He thought that she was just doing undercover intelligence-gathering jobs. He knew nothing about the assassinations. He never watched the news, particularly the international portions.

Alexi felt her motherly instincts kick in and let herself indulge for a moment. "So how are you doing with school? Are you eating anything healthy these days?" He had a tendency to get so involved in his studies and games that he forgot to eat, or simply munched on Fritos and jerky. His small refrigerator usually had a collection of partially rotted food that Alexi periodically tossed out.

"Straight 4.0, ma'm. Taking my vitamins, doing Blimpy's, Taco Bell, Olga's....."

"Stick with Olga's, it's healthier. And try the Greek restaurant by the parking garage behind your favorite bookstore."

"Yes, ma'm. Their *avgolemono* is to die for, I understand."

"You've been talking to your mother again." Chaz' relationship with his mom was an off-again on-again proposition. His mother was an enormous woman who wore huge caftan-type long dresses, a multitude of mis-matched earrings, and was into New Age in a big way. Currently, she was working hard to raise money to send food to the Sudan, and Alexi doubted that she was aware of what her own son was eating.

"We're in communication." Chaz' voice had a tinge of laughter in it. Alexi could appreciate the humor.

Alexi knew that he and his mother usually met at local poetry readings, folk music festivals, or vegetarian restaurants. Chaz had entered the university at age fourteen and lived at home until he was seventeen. He moved out and tried dorm life but it didn't suit him, and he arranged to live in Alexi's apartment.

In a visit with him to his mother's for dinner, Alexi discovered that Chaz had grown up in an old house in Ann Arbor full of cats, papers, cat-hair laden dust bunnies, half-eaten food rotting on countertops, unwashed dishes, bunches of herbs hanging from the ceilings, crystals dangling in every window, clothing lying around in piles, and countless objects of interest that amounted to a

New Age contemporary artifact collection. A stereo was usually turned up at high volume, playing music of Arlo Guthrie, Pete Seeger or Joan Baez, or synthesizer music that wafted through the three floors of the old building. The roof leaked, the cellar was full of debris, and the place smelled like old socks with a touch of sandalwood.

Alexi respected his need for his own space. His mother never walked up to his apartment, due to her weight and knees that didn't tolerate long stair climbs.

"Just checking, kid."

"Just fine, ma'm."

She mentally shook herself out of the conversation. "So do you think a search is possible?" She shouldn't ask. But he was so good at it. "Don't want to compromise you....." She was always worried that someone would find Chaz and prosecute him, as what he was doing was highly questionable, if not illegal. Well, actually, it *was* primarily illegal.

"Can do. I've got nothing really important for the next few hours...."

"Be really really really careful, kid. Play it close. Don't leave any little danglers."

"No way, ma'm."

"Good! Catch you later."

After Alexi hung up, she realized that any kind of sleep was impossible. Just time for a brief rest before she went to dinner with Jim.

The undercurrent of anger with Neil and his training exercise for new surveillance employees came to the surface again. She grabbed a pillow from the bed and threw it across the room. "Damn you!" Then the image of the mime with the gun popped up and she wondered what would have happened if Powder Horn Lady hadn't stepped in and saved her ass. Maybe having some kind of backup wasn't a bad idea.

Chapter 23 - J.R. at the Mask

The brief rest turned into a two-hour nap. She dreamed about Joe Pelloni wrapped in gold cloth, standing on a box next to the Trevi Fountain. He was wearing a King Tut headdress, his face exposed. The mime was shooting at him. Alexi was running toward Joe, trying to put herself between him and the shooter to protect him, but she was too late, and when the figure wrapped in gold bent over, it just kept on going, down and down. Her legs were heavy as though weighted with lead. She had to protect Joe. No. She had to make sure he was dead. Kill him with a big powder horn she threw, and it moved in slow motion, arcing over and over...

She woke up, feeling sweat running down her face. Protecting Joe? Killing Joe? She showered and dressed in black slacks and a turquoise blouse, applied makeup and added turquoise earrings. Wear the vest? No. Bullet-proof, but if a shooter aimed anywhere else, it wouldn't do much good.

This time, she placed a tell-tale tiny piece of paper behind one of the hinges of the door as she exited, so that if anyone came in her room, she would know it, and a Do Not Disturb sign in three languages on the outside doorknob. Her tracker on Jim showed him near the Tiber, probably already there.

A taxi pulled up in front of the hotel as she exited, but she shook her head at the driver and started walking. Too convenient. She walked a block and took a right turn onto a one-way street coming toward her, knowing the taxi had not had enough time to turn around. Another taxi came down the one-way, and she flagged it down.

The ride to the restaurant took longer than she expected. A doorman stood under a short awning at the plain exterior, a sign *THE MASK* was displayed at the entrance. It appeared safe enough.

Jim Russell had a crooked smile as she approached and he gestured for a chair on his left, which she suspected was his good side for hearing. He looked a bit better than he had earlier.

"I had a nap this afternoon, how about you?" She put her bag on the floor at her feet, keeping the pocket with the gun within easy reach.

"Oh, yes, so did I. Seems like I have to keep recharging my batteries." He kept the hand that trembled under the table. After the experience at the Trevi, she thought of the possibility that he could be holding a gun on his lap under the table. No. Not here. But why was she here? It seemed less and less that he was her target. Yet she felt there was something more that she should do. What was it? Well, she had to eat something.

They ordered drinks. He talked about the Palatine. "I'd like to go up there again one last time. Today I sent my finished manuscript to my friend at the university press. There is already an agreement to publish."

"Wonderful!" She picked up her drink - clear creme de menthe and creme de cacao in case the meal was too spicy. Her stomach appreciated the soothing coating beforehand.

"I agreed to have him as editor, and I am primary author. He's kind of acting as a ghost writer with credits in case I made mistakes. I won't be around long enough to see it published."

"Have you been working on this for very long?" Alexi asked.

"Years, actually. We get together sometimes, but mostly by phone or e-mail." He took a long drink of whiskey and water. He reached into his pocket and she dropped her hand toward her gun. He pulled out a small box and laid it on the table in front of her. She put her hand back on the table.

"What's this?" Alexi reached out and picked up the box. It was made of some kind of wood, perforated in a geometric design. Something inside rattled as she shook it slightly.

"Key to a safe deposit box. The instructions and location in there." He looked directly into her eyes and she saw his pain and a question. "You know I don't have any family. Probably won't be able to get back to the box to take care of things.

Figured you're an honest person. Just don't trust those other yay-hoos back in the States."

"Jim... I don't know what to say, except that I'm honored that you trust me." With what? She had no idea what was in Jim Russell's safety deposit box, where in the world it was, or what he expected her to do with the contents. What she did realize was that he was much sicker than she had thought, very little time to take care of whatever was in the box.

The waiter interrupted with menus and a basket of warm bread. Jim picked up his menu and opened it. Evidently their conversation would resume after they ordered. Alexi began reading the entrees aloud, trying to lighten the conversation.

"This food is all Sicilian! Great!" She saw several of her favorites and then came to the last entree. "Wait a minute... horsemeat? Had that once. Unintended."

Jim grinned and laughed "Ha!" - one of his short barks that made a man at the next table half turn around and look at him. "It's a Sicilian specialty."

"Well, I don't *think* so!" Alexi appreciated the reprieve from having to talk about his request.

After the waiter was gone Alexi had already forgotten what she had ordered. She waited for Jim to resume their conversation and looked at the decorations. The walls were dark with the recessed lighting. There were perhaps two dozen masks on the walls around the room, painted in different colors, with curious shapes. She didn't know if they were Sicilian in origin or came from different countries. Before she could comment about them, Jim began speaking.

"Why you, Elaine? Because I seldom come in contact with anyone like you. Most of the people I've met through my work are only in it for the money. You can't trust them to do anything unless there is something in it for them. Like most people, unfortunately. You'll be compensated, of course." He pulled a small piece of bread out of the basket. "I probably seem like a bitter old man, but I've had too many experiences."

"I guess I suspected that." Alexi poured some olive oil into her bread plate and sprinkled a liberal amount of salt on it.

They dipped the crusty bread in the oil. The man had made a strange request. Was she being set up?

Alexi finally spoke. "When did you get the plastic surgery on your face?" Would his story match up with her intel on him?

"Korean War. Burned mostly on my body, some on my face. They fixed it up as good as they could, but there were more procedures later."

"I'm sorry, Jim." Yes. The story matched.

"Over and done with, babe. I was lucky, though. Kept the use of most of me, anyway. Not much to look at, but you make do with what you've got. Hey, this place is a good choice!" He gestured at the masks on the walls. "I've got to look better than the decorations."

Alexi appreciated his joke and laughed with him. The waiter came with their dinners, and she noticed that Jim wasn't eating much. He ordered another large whiskey and water, drank it and ordered another. She barely tasted her food.

The small box sat in front of them on the table, unopened.

"You never told me about your research project, Jim."

"I guess I didn't." The gaunt white-haired man pushed his plate a bit away from him, and picked up his glass with his good hand. The hand that trembled lay beside his plate, and he didn't bother to hide it.

"So...." She smiled at him gently.

"I'll have to take you back a bit. When I was young the Catholic church was a big part of my life. Went to Catholic schools, served as an altar boy in the church." He grimaced. "The nuns were strict, of course, that was common. But the priests...." He looked away.

"Oh. You were one of the boys that were...."

"Molested. Yes, you could say that."

"Once? More?" She felt slightly sick.

"Repeatedly. For years."

"And now?"

"My research searched for patterns, justifications, words used that do not explicitly spell out what has been done through the ages, but clearly define a history of abuse over centuries."

"I'm so sorry about what happened to you, Jim. Is the research helping? With what you must have been carrying with you all these years?"

"Yes. Tremendously. But I ran out of time." He looked directly at her again. "I finished what I could of the Vatican research. There could be more, but it will have to be done by someone else. I've had to pinch it off, but there is enough. More than enough. And I do have a sense of closure." He sighed deeply.

Alexi had built her own life after the years with her father. What she was doing now seemed meaningful and important. Was she just making up for the earlier abuse, getting revenge for the childhood? She always heard her father's voice accusing her of being a coward just before she killed a bad guy. And the sense of release afterward, proving that she wasn't a coward... Was that her real motivation? She pulled herself back from her own questions, and concentrated again on Jim's more immediate concerns.

"And now what?" She looked in his eyes. Saw pain and something else.

"I've tied up all the loose ends but this." He pointed at the small box. "One last thing to take care of before I depart."

She looked at the small box sitting on the table between them.

"Please open it." He pushed it toward her.

The top of the box fit tightly. Inside only a folded piece of paper and a key. Tiny writing. She got her reading glasses from her bag, unfolded the paper and turned it slightly in the dim light so that she could see the words.

Alexi looked up at Jim with raised eyebrows.

"The street address of the bank in New York City and the numbers needed for the safety deposit box. I have already contacted them and gave them permission for you to remove the contents of the box." Jim said.

"What is in it?"

"A portfolio and other papers. Bonds, CDs, some gold bars. Authorization for you to dispose of it the way I want. After talking with my lawyer and figuring out what he would do with

114

it, I decided on this as an alternative. Kind of a last minute decision. As you can see, babe, I'm not gonna be using it."

"What? Me? I don't know, Jim. I've never done..." Oh my God. He trusted ditsy Elaine. "What do you want done with it?"

"There's an organization that deals with abuses of the Church to children. Instructions are in there with pertinent information. I already sent documents appointing you executor if you accept the responsibility, but you will have to sign the papers with the bank. I want all the funds to go to the organization except the amount given to you as executor. It's a substantial amount, Elaine. I've already sent a document to the organization telling them you will be contacting them and that the money is theirs."

"You already..." Alexi straightened in her chair. Amazing. The audacity of the man. Just assuming that she would comply with his wishes.

"If you decided tonight not to do it, I've got another letter appointing my attorney."

Alexi felt a surge of relief. He wasn't completely bonkers. He had thought it out. Doing what he asked wouldn't compromise her. It was a simple enough thing to do. The man must have no one in his life, not even his colleague.

"Will you?" He bent slightly toward her, and she recognized the intensity of his request.

"Yes. I can do that, Jim. But what will you do? Where will you go?"

"I thought perhaps a last walk up the Palatine, tomorrow morning. There is nothing at my hotel now that is of any value. They can keep it." He paused. "The little garden, babe, you know... I plan to do it there."

She couldn't meet his eyes this time, and looked away. This was coming too fast. It didn't fit the profile she had originally imagined for him. His request came too quickly. She didn't know him well. She shouldn't trust him or anyone. Good grief! The man was going to do himself in. Tomorrow morning.

"If you want to..." He was asking her to be there. She felt like someone had hit her in the gut.

"Wouldn't you rather be alone?"

"No." His voice was so low she almost didn't hear it. "But it could compromise you. the Italian police are very thorough. So perhaps you shouldn't."

Alexi thought about the times she had effectively disappeared after one of her jobs. "I'll do as you ask about the safety deposit box. Don't worry about your money; I have enough of my own. But about tomorrow, I'll think about it." She refolded the paper, placed it back in the box, and put the box in her bag. Elaine Birdsall could go to New York. Her alternate identification would pass at the bank.

The waiter came to the table with the check. Jim paid quickly. He finished his drink, and Alexi finished hers. They stood up to leave. He adjusted his jacket and tie, straightened his shoulders slightly, and walked slowly ahead of her.

"I'll be at the garden around seven o'clock." They stood near the curb waiting for a taxi. He clutched a post holding up the awning over the entrance and his profile was dark against the lights of the restaurant window. The streetlights gave a soft glow to the area, another image that would remain for a while in her memory.

She lifted her arm to flag down a taxi. Then she decided. "I'll meet you there, Jim."

"Take the cab, babe. I'm going to take a walk before I go back to my hotel." He reached out and touched her face gently. "Thanks."

She got in the cab without looking back. He didn't want her to know where he was staying because she might try to stop him. He was too weak to take a walk. Probably catch another taxi. She was appalled at the promises she had given this man, and hoped she wouldn't regret it.

Another thought hit her and filled her with a deep sense of sadness. Joe Pelloni had to be Stefan Cardini – the Cougar she was to 'take out.'

Chapter 24 - Warnings and sympathy

When Alexi's cab pulled up in front of her hotel, she got out quickly and went inside. There was a small vase of flowers sitting on the front desk, and the clerk called to her as she walked past.

"These came for you, signora." He picked up the vase and held it out to her.

"Grazie." She took the vase off the counter. It was heavy, weighted with something.

"Prego, signora. Buona sera." He turned back to the small television behind the desk to watch a soccer game.

Alexi went to her room, checked the tell-tale and found it in place. She put the vase on the bathroom counter and lifted out the flowers. As promised, there was a small box of shell cartridges wrapped in plastic. She took the gun from her bag and checked the shells against the ones already in the gun. They matched.

She checked the room again for bugs, found none, decided to try to get some sleep and called the front desk for an early wake-up call.

Her cell phone rang as she was getting into bed. Neil.

"Got problems." There was no crunching on his end, and he sounded serious.

"What?" She sat up on the edge of the bed, bare feet on the carpeting.

"Your Kling-on from the plane?"

"Yes." The dork in the suit. She had used the Red Hat ladies to escape him.

"Turns out he's not what he seemed. Credentials checked out, but got word that he's been working both sides of the street."

"What the hell?" She knew her target was supposed to be an old ex-assassin. Was Cardini working for someone or working for himself? She was already convinced from the intel that he wasn't senile. He wanted to screw up the peace process. He was the other side. But what?

"Like what other side Neil?" She stood up, suddenly feeling alert.

"We think that he was working with the people that bugged your room, and the guy that tried to shoot you. They're onto you.

Want you to get out of there as soon as possible." More silence. Yes. Dead serious.

"What about the target? Let him go ahead? Don't stop him?"

"We're pretty sure now that it is that guy Pelloni, even if he checks out ok. Could be a really good plastic surgery."

"Yeah, I've been having some doubts about him. He cut out pretty quick when that mime showed up. If it hadn't been for Elli...."

"She's free-lance. Not actually one of ours, just a kind of sub-contract arrangement."

"Oh. Like me. What about the gypsies?"

"They're ours. Been with us for a while, you can trust them."

"Thanks." But no thanks. This entire job was a disaster.

"I've got trackers on them, sending you the numbers now. Hold on." She forwarded the information with her computer and then picked up the phone again.

"Alexi - you've got to get to a safe house. NOW!"

"I can't. There is something I have to do first. Don't worry. Give me instructions to the safe house, Neil." If she could trust a safe house. She had always trusted Neil, but her antenna was up big time on this job.

Alexi tore a piece of paper from a small pad next to the phone and wrote the instructions. While standing next to the desk, she checked the wastebasket for anything she might have put in there. It was empty. The thought crossed her mind how she kept erasing evidence of her existence. She was always erasing herself.

"So are you going over there now?"

She thought about Jim Russell going to the Palatine in the morning. She had promised to be there. He was obviously not the target, and she would have to deal with Pelloni somehow. But she hated to renege on a promise. And there was the small box in her bag.

"I think not, Neil. Perhaps tomorrow." Alexi needed time to plan, time to think, and a better handle on the situation. To cut and run now would leave her without closure, and she had an uncomfortable feeling about not finishing the job she had set out to do.

"Watch your back, 'Lexi." His voice was more than serious now, a rasping quality that showed more emotion than she was used to hearing.

"I will, Neil. I'll call you tomorrow." She hung up and removed the battery from the phone. Tonight she was on her own. To hell with Neil. To hell with Marsden Security. To hell with trying to get some sleep.

Alexi pulled clothes and the blonde wig out of the suitcase and took it all into the bathroom. Washing only took a few minutes, and she rolled all of them in bath towels, pressing out all of the water she could. She got a plastic garbage bag and her hair dryer from her suitcase, placed the damp garments and wig in the bag, poked a hole in the bag with the tip of a pen, fluffed them up some, fastened the hair dryer to the bag with a rubber band and turned it on. Steam started coming out of the bag.

Leaving the clothes and wig drying, she went to her laptop, got on the Internet and pulled up Chaz' encrypted chat room address. If he was on line, her message would pop up immediately. He was on line at all times of the day and night, and whatever time it was in Ann Arbor, he was there.

> *Alexi: So what's happening?*
>
> *Chaz: Not much. You O.K.?*
>
> *Alexi: Fine. Got anything for me?*
>
> *Chaz: Some good stuff. Ready?*
>
> *Alexi: Go for it.*
>
> *Chaz: Russell is for real. Nothing looks like a red flag. Just a bitter old vet with an attitude. Maybe a little crazy, but he's got his reasons.*
>
> *Alexi: I know. So what about the other guy?*
>
> *Chaz: Good cover for him with the feds, but he seems to have gone rogue some time ago, tied up with another outfit. They've been trying to track him down, but he's good at evasion. Original name was Stefan Cardeni. Grew up in Chicago, had grandparents living in southern Illinois. Family hard-line Catholics, he was supposed to grow up to be a priest but opted out. He lived with a guy that was an arms dealer among other things.*
>
> *Alexi: What other things?*
>
> *Chaz: They used international trade in antiques and historic items as a cover. Indication of biochemicals, possibly nuclear. In fact, strong possibility selling nuclears to countries not on the approved list.*
>
> *Alexi: Wow.*

Chaz: Yeah, wow. Also, Cardeni invested his own money in the business.

Alexi: More?

Chaz: He looks like someone with friends and interests in bad places. You've got me worried. Stay away from him – he's bad news. What are you supposed to do?

Alexi: Just get information.

Chaz: Be careful.

Alexi: No prob. I'm covered. Just needed the info.

Chaz: You sure?

Alexi: I'm sure. Hey, check your frig lately for mold?

Chaz: Of course. Green, pink, black.....

Alexi: I'm coming over there the first thing when I get back, kid. With Lysol!

Chaz: But it's so tasty. Hey, I'm thinking of getting wheels.

Alexi: What kind? A tricycle would be nice.....

Chaz: Harley would be nice.

Alexi: Yeah, right. You should be so lucky.

Chaz: Mom has that old Mustang, I could fix that up.

Alexi: Gas prices would eliminate any hope of keeping your apartment. You'd have to move everything into the Mustang, and I don't think it would fit.

Chaz: Guess it will have to be that mountain bike I saw on e-bay.

Alexi: I've got a good bike in the garage you can have.

Chaz: You're on. My bike kind of died on me. Trying to figure out an equation in my head, and ran into a dumpster. Bent the front wheel. It's pretty rusty anyway.

Alexi: Just help yourself, kid. You've got a key.

Chaz: Thanks. Is there anything else?

Alexi: Not now. You're sure you weren't traced getting the intel?

Chaz: No way.

Alexi: Later.

Chaz: Bye.

Alexi got off the Internet, shut down the computer, and went into the bathroom. The big black garbage bag was still inflated, and the hair dryer was still running. She turned it off, reached in the bag for her clothes and the wig and pulled them out. The clothes were nearly dry, the blouse slightly wrinkled, and the wig still damp. She turned the hair dryer back on, held up the wig, ran a brush through it, and dried it quickly.

Alexi thought about Pelloni/Cardini, and cursed herself for being attracted to him. He probably knew who she actually was and what she was hired to do, or if he didn't, it would just be a matter of time. The thing with the mime at the Trevi could have been something he had planned, and explained his quick exit. If he was working for himself, he was a far more formidable target than any she had seen so far.

She had come to Rome alone, hopefully to find an old man who might be confused or twisted, but still dangerous. Trying to eliminate a stone-cold killer working with others was a totally different proposition.

Neil was probably right, but she hated it. She could no longer avoid help, and would have to give in to his demands and work with a team. It was time to accept reality.

She promised Jim Russell that she would be there on the Palatine, and she would. She also had promised to dispense of his assets as he wished, a promise she would keep somehow. Alexi looked at the clock and realized she needed to get some rest. No one had come crashing into her room so far to dispense with her, and if she didn't restore her energy, she wouldn't be able to function.

She moved the desk chair under the doorknob, checked the window lock and convinced herself that none of the air vents near the ceiling could possibly be used to access her room. Going to the tiny refrigerator, she pulled out a small bottle of rum, mixed it with part of a bottle of cola, mixed the two in a bathroom glass and downed it in three swallows. Lying back on the bed, she picked up her Kindle and tried to read while she waited for the alcohol to kick in.

The phone rang and she reached over to answer it. No voice. Automatic alarm. Morning, and she had slept well, thanks to the rum.

She had only one day before the meeting at the Vatican. Today she needed to be at the safe house and work with the Marsdon Security team. Not yet.

The morning ritual was done in minutes. Now, only the matter of meeting Jim on the Palatine. She did need to store her suitcase some place where she could get it later. Leaving it at the desk was not an option. Someone might check. Cardini wasn't working alone.

Alexi went through her usual procedures in the room, wiped down everything, and left nothing behind. She wadded up the towels and washcloths, took them into the hallway, and left them outside the door of another room. Checked her shoulder bag one last time for essentials and made sure the small wooden box was in an inside zipped pocket. She quickly scarfed down breakfast and left the room key on the desk.

The outside exit used by hotel employees led into an alley. Alexi walked quickly to the end, hailed a taxi, got in, and asked the driver to take her to a hotel near the Tiber. She checked in and left her bag to be picked up later.

Since no one appeared to be carrying out surveillance, she walked casually down the street. Her shoulder bag was heavy with the laptop, cell phone, knitting, gun, cartridges, and other essentials. A money belt under her clothes held her Elaine Birdsall identification and passport, and some cash. The tracker showed that Jim Russell was already on the Palatine.

Another taxi took her to the entrance, and the walk up the slope seemed a bit more difficult than on her previous visit, probably because of the weight of the shoulder bag. Thank goodness for comfortable shoes.

Toward the top she found a bench and sank down on it, letting the bag drop beside her. Definitely time to replace the laptop. Nope. No longer a spring chicken. Shrugged off the thought. She got to her feet, slung the bag over her shoulder again, and made her way up the worn steps of tufa past descendants of plants that had grown there for thousands of years. Alexi stopped at the little staircase leading down to the small garden. The overgrown tufa stones of the wall were shadowed by the branches of the trees, and she could see Jim Russell sitting in the same spot as before, arms stretched out along the back of the bench.

"Hi." She sat beside him. He reached out and lightly touched her on the shoulder.

"Didn't think you'd come." His voice was low. She turned to look at him and saw that his pallor was worse, probably from the climb up the hill.

"Wouldn't miss it."

"Beautiful day, babe."

"Perfect day." She took out the knitting case and laid it beside her on the bench.

"So you're making socks for your grandson." He looked away. "Never had kids, so no grandkids."

"Sorry, Jim." Following the plan she had made earlier, she pulled one of the long Number 2 needles from the case and laid it beside her on the bench. "So what's next?"

"This." He reached in his jacket pocket. The trembling hand came out with a small gun. There was no silencer on the end.

"I think it will be kind of noisy. You know?" She looked over at him, and he nodded. "Could be a better way."

"Don't have any pills that would do the job. Just the ones for the leukemia, and the ones for pain, but they don't do much." He laughed; the sharp harsh sound that she knew probably came from some kind of throat injury. She wondered if it was from the time in Korea or from a priest forcing him to perform some kind of oral sex act.

"'So, no pills."

"Nope, babe. No pills. Just this." He put the gun back in his pocket. Not quite ready.

"I promised to take care of your assets, do what you wanted. I will. I keep my promises."

"Thanks, babe. I figured." He pulled out the gun again and started playing with it, twirling it around the finger of his good hand. She wondered if he had any idea of how to kill himself or if he was just playing with the idea like he was playing with the gun.

"Watch out, you'll hurt yourself!" she said and then started laughing. He laughed too, his own harsh croaking.

"Wouldn't that be a hoot!" he said, and that started them laughing again. Remembering why they were there, she calmed quickly. They sat quietly for a moment, not speaking. A small bird flew down to the rough stone wall beside them. Jim cradled the gun in both hands and sat looking down at it.

"I can help." Alexi picked up the knitting needle.

"Kind of wondered how you could knit with one needle." He laid the gun on the bench beside him.

"It's a magic knitting needle." She pulled up on the top that had a large 2 imprinted on it. A slim ceramic point slid out of the pointed tip. She cradled the entire syringe in her hands carefully. "It has a magic potion inside."

Jim Russell looked down at her hands and the syringe. "What kind of magic potion? Something to make me fall in love with a beautiful woman? Something to make me dream?" He looked over at her smiling, his features arranged in an approximation of one of the grotesque masks in the restaurant the night before.

"Not that, just an easy slipping away with nothing left behind except an indication of a heart attack." She spoke quietly, waiting.

"You are incredible, Elaine Birdsall, or whatever your name is. Who are you? Why do I trust you? I never trust people. I don't think I've ever met anyone like you. Are you some kind of angel sent here to help out an old reprobate?"

"Maybe you've been watching too many movies on TV, Jim. I'm no angel. Just a woman from the States. Sent here to do a job. Got waylaid by a man that intrigued me. This is part of my kit so that I can keep a bad guy from hurting a lot of people."

"My God! Who is he?" Jim leaned back and picked up the gun again. For an instant, Alexi felt a sharp stab of fear that he would point it at her. That she was wrong about him not being Cardini. No. She shoved the thought aside.

In the next minutes, Alexi told him a short version of what was happening. She knew he only half believed her. It was too bizarre for anyone to accept so quickly. He had his own concerns. She knew he could probably never make it up the Palatine again. She didn't tell him who she really was, or about the company. Just a thumbnail sketch of reality, and then repeated her offer to help him.

"You sure aren't what I thought you were. Nobody ever is. Do you have any credentials? Maybe this is some kind of trick. Maybe the Vatican…"

"Want to see my credentials?" She started rummaging in her bag.

"No, don't bother."

"I don't carry a badge or anything…"

"Okay, babe. I believe you. Strange kind of angel. You gonna use that thing on the bad guy?" He nodded toward the knitting needle.

"Will it hurt?"

"Just a tiny poke."

Jim turned to her, and she saw tears in his eyes. She reached out for him, and the gun fell to the ground as she wrapped her arms around his frail body. He sobbed then, his face in her shoulder, horrible harsh sounds that came from his throat and reverberated deep in his chest. She held him close for a few minutes and then he sat up and pulled back. He blew his nose and wiped his eyes on a wad of tissue.

"Change your mind?" she asked gently.

"No. Let's do it, babe." He pulled back his sleeve, exposing an arm that was pale and withered. The veins stood out in blue lines. There were small red and blue bruises where the surface arteries had broken. She found a vein easily. Her own heart was pounding now, and she took a deep breath.

The needle went in and she pushed on the plunger. He looked at her once and then fell over sideways onto the bench. She pulled down his sleeve. With the bruises already on his arm the pin-prick of the needle wouldn't be noticed. Alexi picked up his gun and put it in her bag with the knitting needle case.

She stood looking down at the old white-haired man lying on his side on the bench, bent over and closed his eyes gently. Her heart was pounding, her throat tightly closed. With one breath, she released the anguish that had been like a wild animal trapped inside. A deep moan escaped, and she didn't even try to stop the tears blurring her vision and running down her cheeks.

"Ah, Jim. Rest well." Her voice was harsh and barely above a whisper.

She could still feel her heart beating and her breathing was fast and shallow. Walking back up the few steps to the path was like plowing through sand. The tears were coming now, and she wondered why she felt this, when before with the others there had been nothing. She hadn't heard that horrid word her father said. Always before, she heard it. But not this time.

She walked down the hill to the street below, the trees and sky blurring like a Monet painting. Wiping her eyes on her sleeve, she stepped out into a sunlit street and found a taxi stand. There was a telephone and a small wooden bench. She put her bag on the bench, and dug out her cell.

Alexi asked the desk clerk at the hotel where she wouldn't be staying to send her bag to the restaurant across the street from where she now stood. She had to leave immediately for home. Put it on the credit card she had used to register. Include a tip for himself. He was glad to accommodate, and if she ever was in Roma again, please stay at the hotel.

She closed the phone and walked across the street to a restaurant. It appeared that no one had followed her, but she wasn't sure. She wasn't hungry but could use a stiff drink. The emotional reaction to what she had done was insane. Was she losing her edge? She needed to get herself together. It was still too early to go to the Pantheon to meet Pelloni/Cardini. If he still would meet her. It might be her only chance to stop him.

Alexi used a stall in the restaurant bathroom to make preparations. She took out the knitting case again and used her hidden jacket sleeve pockets to prepare herself for the meeting, one small needle with a nerve deadening agent, another contained the same solution she had used up on the Palatine.

She wiped any prints from the gun she took from Jim Russell, wrapped it in a paper towel and dropped it in the back of the toilet in the bathroom where it wouldn't be found immediately.

The gun taken from the mime went in her pocket where she could pull it out easily, or just shoot through the fabric of her slacks. Her jacket came down over the pocket and hid the bulge.

Alexi went out of the bathroom, finished her drink, and saw a taxi pull up in front. The driver got out and looked around, and she went out to greet him.

"Your suitcase, signora?" He opened the back door of the taxi and pulled the case from the back seat.

"Grazie! No. Just put it back. I need to go somewhere."

"The airport? Train?" The driver's English was adequate but somewhat difficult to understand. She gave him the address of the safe house.

Leaving the Palatine behind, she leaned back against the seat of the taxi and tried to forget the little garden and the man lying on a bench surrounded by beauty.

Chapter 25 – Quick thinking

Alexi waited in the taxi while the driver took her suitcase to the door. She sat on the far side of the back seat away from the building so that the person answering the door couldn't see her. The driver came back and got in, grunting slightly. He was a large man, and his belly brushed against the steering wheel. He looked at her in the mirror.

"Now where do you want to go, signora?" His spoke English with an accent that sounded Eastern European, perhaps Russian or Polish.

"The Pantheon, per favore." She leaned back against the seat, trying to will herself to relax as the taxi pulled away from the curb. Turning slightly, she looked out the back window and then at the outside mirrors on the taxi. It didn't appear that anyone had been following, but she couldn't be sure.

Joe said he would meet her at the ancient building. She brushed her hand over the blonde wig, and checked her makeup in a small mirror from her bag. Presentable. The deadly short needles were already in the sleeves of her jacket. Alexi kept the gun in her pocket and fingered the safety to make sure it was on and the cartridge clip in place.

"I need something to eat. Can you pull over long enough for me to get something from a food vendor?"

It only took a moment, and she was back in the taxi with two sandwiches and two cans of soda. She handed a sandwich and soda over the seat to the driver.

He looked at her in the rear-view mirror and she saw only the upper part of his face, his eyes crinkling in a smile.

"Grazie, signora."

"Prego." She ate the sandwich quickly and washed it down with the cola. No point in spending a lot of time. Not planning on a long lunch date.

She got out of the taxi, slung the heavy bag over her shoulder, and felt a twinge in her knees from the climb up the Palatine. Checking the area, she saw only the usual tourists and traffic, small trucks blocking the street as they were unloaded at shops around the piazza, and the usual scooters, bicycles and small automobiles that seemed to follow no pattern. The pedestrians appeared focused on wherever they were heading, and she didn't see anyone just loitering. No other taxis in her vicinity. The tracker showed Pelloni some distance away.

Of course, if he was meeting her here, he would have had any associate already in place. The usual vendors were in the piazza - Africans with blankets on the ground loaded with cheap fake-leather purses, an Asian woman selling small mechanical cats that crept along the ground and flipped over, another dark-haired woman with a basket of flowers that was going from table to table at one of the outside restaurants, a gypsy playing a guitar sat by the fountain in the center of the piazza with his hat on the cobblestones in front of him for money.

She went past the huge bronze doors into the Pantheon, looking up for a second at the oculus in the ceiling. The sun was high now, and a beam of light came down into the enormous round room and struck the floor. She looked around the niches with small groups of tourists clustered at the various alcoves with statues and paintings. Raphael's tomb was on her left, and the tourists seemed to be moving around the room counter-clockwise. Alexi moved that way also, not wanting to stand out.

She was beginning to think he wouldn't show and hid her irritation as the tour guide droned on about how the building designed by Hadrian had been built in 67 B.C. as a pagan temple, but most of the pagan statues had been removed and replaced by Christian statuary and paintings, and that two Italian kings were buried in the building.

Alexi moved with the group of Americans until they stopped at the burial place of Umberto I, and then she walked slowly away from them. She still had not seen Pelloni/Cardini, and wondered if he was going to make the appointment. She checked her phone ap and saw that he was approaching.

Just as she reached the Raphael burial spot, she saw him coming in the doorway. He looked around the room and waved when he saw her. Wearing a soft black leather jacket over a white turtleneck sweater, and dark pants, with his white hair and handsome face, he was a striking contrast to the casually dressed, overweight American tourists of the tour group.

"Elaine! Sorry I'm late!" He smiled as she came toward him, and she felt a slight constriction in her chest. Knowing that now he was her target made it difficult to maintain the required hardness.

"I was enjoying the tour. No problem."

"Do you want to continue, or would you like some tea?" He stood there looking at her, and the warmth that had been there before was gone. He knew who she was; she was certain of it now. He smiled, but the smile didn't reach his eyes.

"A cup of tea would be wonderful!"

She followed him out into the sunshine past the huge, nearly 2,000 year old heavily decorated bronze door. The vendors came toward them, holding out their wares, and they had to avoid stepping on a small battery-operated yellow metal car that was spinning around, operated by a remote control in the hand of a small Asian vendor. Joe brushed the vendors aside impatiently. Then he turned to her and smiled. Not his usual smile. His mouth turned down somewhat and his head jerked back.

"Like cockroaches, aren't they?" He led the way across the piazza to a restaurant. She walked beside him, feeling his hand on her arm just above the elbow, and a slight chill ran through her.

She wondered who would come at her with a gun this time, perhaps one of the vendors. There were no mimes, no mummy wrapped in gold cloth, only the gypsy violinist standing by the fountain. Not the gypsy from Detroit. She looked sideways at the gypsy, a small dark complexioned man wearing dark pants, white shirt and a black vest. He had short, dark curly hair, and a bright red scarf was tied around his neck. He was playing the violin but was too far away for her to hear it.

Joe led her to the same restaurant where they had been before, and held her chair for her as she sat down with her back to one of the dormant heating units. A large square green umbrella shaded the table from the sun. He sat down on her left. Using her left hand would put her at a disadvantage if she intended to make a move, although she had practiced using both hands.

"So how's the research coming along, Joe?" She remembered to be Elaine Birdsall and tried the ditsy dame persona, but it was getting difficult. Her stomach had started to knot up, and she made herself take in a long, slow deep breath. The gun was heavy against her hip in the pocket of her slacks on the right side. She could feel the small tube inside her right sleeve, and cursed herself for not putting it in on the left. The paralytic was on the left.

"Oh, I've finished nearly everything," he said. "The journal stuff has been fascinating, but there are some things I need to check out at other archives." He didn't look at her, and she now wondered if he had actually been doing any research, or just using that as a cover to get into buildings. Why the archives? With the strict security systems, she doubted library access would provide what he needed to get close to the meeting participants if they were using a conference room in another part of the complex.

"That's great. You must have a sense of accomplishment."

"Yes. Now I can move on to other things." He seemed more formal in his conversation, and less interested in charming her.

The waiter took their orders, and he asked for the house red wine. Her tea and his glass of wine came quickly, and she opened the tea bag packet and dropped a small sachet-type bag of black tea into the hot water in her cup. She picked up a small slice of lemon and sprinkled salt on the center of it, sucked on the tart and salt for a moment. Then she sprinkled sugar on the rind and ate the rind, chewing and swallowing it quickly.

"I never saw anyone do that before," he said. He held his wine glass with both hands and looked at her, not saying anything more.

She realized that she had probably been keeping her hands busy because she was a bit nervous. She took out the sachet tea bag, and squeezed it slightly, cleaning the lemon juice from her fingers, and laid it on the saucer. Blowing a little bit across the cup, she took a sip.

"My kids always did that when they were young, and now the grandkids do it. And me." She smiled and took another sip of her tea. "They all prefer lemons to ice cream - go figure! The kids will ask for a dish of lemon slices and go through the whole routine." She had heard this from a friend in Ann Arbor and used the story before.

"That's incredible!" This time the smile reached his eyes, and he drank some of the wine.

"You can never predict what children will come up with. Always a surprise." She saw the gypsy violinist pick up his hat, take out money and put it in his pants pocket. Something about his movements reminded her of the mime putting money in his baggy pants. She reached in her pocket slowly; making sure the safety was off on the gun. The thin needle in her right sleeve would be difficult to use, but the one her left could disable Cardini and give her enough time to switch over to the right.

"So are you going back to the Vatican library again?" she asked.

"No. I'm done there, for now. Just have a few things to wrap up. I might go to the other archives, but I think I covered most of it in St. Louis. They may have other material here, though." He shrugged, and she was certain that the intensity of his interest that the convincing line he had fed her about the letters and documents was false.

They talked about the Pantheon, the weather, and he ordered food. Alexi declined, keeping an eye on the gypsy near the fountain. The waiter brought him a plate of pasta with chicken and more wine. She had a refill of her tea. Taking out *this* old man in a public place would be tricky, if she could do it at all.

She thought about him telling her his family was Catholic, and the information Chaz had provided. She wondered if Cardini had experienced things with the priests that had created the inner anger she had seen in Jim Russell. For an instant, she thought about the gaunt man lying on the bench in the Palatine garden.

Knowing what she did now about Cardini, she realized she would probably never find out anything about his true past, his childhood, or what had created a person like him. There had to be a serious incident or series of incidents that had made him the person that was today. Charming and warm, attractive even in advancing age, and with a quality that drew her to him. But inside was a man hardened and cruel, who had committed acts so violent that it was hard to equate them with the person sitting next to her. Also, he probably knew who she really was, and was keeping her close to him so that she could be stopped from having any part in preventing him from carrying out his plan. She slowly drew in a deep breath.

Then the thought crossed her mind like a shooting star. She was also a person like Cardini, and in some ways similar to Jim Russell. She carried around past loss and pain. The anger that emanated from it was part of what drove her to carry out the killings she had done.

She could be charming like Cardeni - but had an interior hard enough to be able to kill. And enjoy the killing? Justified with their own view of right and wrong. Cardeni saw the upcoming meeting as a barrier to something important. Just as she had a reason to eliminate him, to prevent him from actions that would compromise something she felt important.

Alexi wished for an instant that she could talk about this with Cardini and then gave herself a mental shake. How long had she been sitting there without speaking? He was looking at her with a slight scowl, and then rearranged his face into a slight smile.

"Would you like a dessert?" His voice lifted her out of her thoughts, although she knew it had only been seconds.

"No. Thank you." She smiled at him and thought how it could have been to meet a nice man in Rome and have the beginning of a real friendship. She had not exactly been alone these past years, but a real relationship wasn't part of her world.

The gypsy violinist was coming toward the table. She felt a strong tightening of her gut and a chill ran up the back of her neck. The gypsy stopped to play for a few minutes, held out his hat for tips, and then moved closer to them.

"Excuse me. Need to...." She got up, put her bag over her shoulder, and walked quickly to the women's bathroom as the gypsy violinist approached their restaurant. Once in the narrow stall, she pulled down her slacks, being careful not to dump the gun on the floor, and urinated. The whole business had unnerved her.

Sitting there for a moment, she realized that the safety was off on the gun, and that she could have shot herself just having a pee. Sweet. Cursing her carelessness, she stood up, arranged her clothing, rearranged the gun, and slipped the safety back on. Perhaps the violinist would be gone by the time she got back to the table.

She took rearranged the wig. A bit of lipstick went on quickly. She straightened her shoulders, and went out into the restaurant.

The gypsy was now at the next restaurant, and she saw that Cardini had laid some money on the table to pay for their lunch.

"Here, let me!" She reached in her bag for her wallet as she sat down, resting her bag on her lap.

"No. I've got it." He stood up, and she also rose from her chair. Her moment had passed. Too late now to make a move. "I can call a cab, is there some place you would like to go?" He looked distracted or disappointed.

She knew she had somehow disrupted his plans, but was surprised that another attempt like that of the day before had been tried. The gypsy was probably the mime at the Trevi, working with him. Perhaps they thought that a repeat of the previous attempt would point at someone who had targeted her. She was sure Cardini would have disappeared as soon as her body was left lying next to the table at the restaurant.

"No. I think I'll just do a bit of shopping first. It's been really nice. Good luck with your research."

"Is there some way I can get in touch with you?" He reached inside his jacket and she felt a sharp chill, but he pulled out a pen and a small notebook. "Phone number back home? Address? E-mail?"

"Do you ever go to Michigan?" she asked.

He seemed nervous. "Not usually, but I could."

Alexi gave him a telephone number that was a Lansing area code and an East Lansing address, both in the Elaine identification and didn't exist. "My e-mail is being changed; I'm really tired of getting so much spam. So when I get back, I'm not going to use the same server."

"Well, here's my card. Just give me a call before you leave, or e-mail me when you get back home." He had written down her information, and put the notebook and pen back in an inner pocket. He took out his wallet, pulled out a small business card and handed it to her. She took it with her left hand and put it in her left slacks pocket, keeping her right hand available for the gun.

"Thanks. Maybe I will." The card was probably fake, and she wondered if the cell phone number was real. Probably not. Well, at least she could track him.

She walked away without looking back, leaving him at the restaurant. It was simply too public for her to make any moves, and she knew that she had been in danger just coming to meet him. The gypsy was obviously a part of his operation, and she wondered how many fake gypsies there were in Rome.

Alexi needed to get to the safe house. She walked feeling as though she had a target on her back. There was a toy store a few shops down from the restaurant and she wound her way past displays of dolls, building blocks and remote-controlled trucks and cars. Turning so that she could see the street in front of the shop, she saw only the light traffic allowed at the edges of the piazza and the usual tourists and pedestrians.

There was a tiny Harley Davidson motorcycle on a display. For Chaz. She bought it, went to the door of the shop and checked out the piazza. Stepping out into the sunshine, she looked around as though deciding where to go next. Traffic was light and several taxis were sat in a row around the corner. The Pantheon was a popular tourist spot, and another taxi pulled up at the end of the line as she walked toward the taxi at the front.

The driver was leaning on the vehicle smoking a cigarette. He opened the door for her and she slid in on a vinyl seat, smelling smoke and stale food. His identification over the visor gave his name as John Patel and his accent sounded as though he were from India. He spoke English with the intonation she recognized and kept up a running patter of talk. Alexi didn't feel like talking, and wanted to get to the safe house as soon as possible. She primarily responded with single grunts and sounds of agreement, and was relieved when they pulled up in front of the building. She tipped the man generously, got out and went up the steps. She didn't look back, glad that the door opened before she reached it and stepped inside.

She stood in the entry of the safe house hating herself. The meeting with Cardini had made her feel vulnerable, weak like her father said. Kudoz. A coward. Ran for the ladies room. Softened up by the thing with Jim Russell. Maybe she wouldn't have another good opportunity. Maybe it was too late to stop him.

Chapter 26 – Thwarted

Stefan Cardeni met the fake gypsy violinist on the street behind the Pantheon. They stood on the shady side of the street in front of a store, speaking in the Kurdish dialect. It was unlikely that their conversation would be understood if it was overheard.

"It was your fault, Stefan. I was all set, and then she got up..." His face was dark with rage.

"I know. Nothing I could do. You will be paid half anyway, of course."

"Only half? That was not the arrangement." He let the violin drop down at his side, and looked both ways. "That stupid woman took my gun. Look at this!" He gestured toward his head. There was a knot from being bashed with the powder horn, partially covered with his thick, curly dark hair. Obviously, he expected compensation.

"I have the money in my room. Just come with me. I will pay you something extra for the head. The woman is been a problem."

They walked around the corner, down a short street, and into an alley behind several tall buildings. Cardeni led the way to a service door into his hotel he had previously propped open slightly with a piece of wood. They went down a short garbage-smelling hallway around a corner to a service elevator. The walls were stained and dirty, the floor of the hallway crusted with an accumulation of grime.

Cardeni punched the 'up' arrow at the elevator and they waited while the lights above the doors showed that it was approaching. The small man next to him banged the violin in a staccato of nervousness. Stefan looked straight ahead, not speaking.

Before the elevator arrived, Stefan stepped quickly behind the shorter man in a single movement grabbed him around the neck. He put one hand on the side of the man's head. The Kurd dropped his violin and reached up to grasp Cardeni's arm that now held him so tightly that his feet barely touched the floor. He put his other hand on the side of the man's head, pushed and twisted. There was a crack of bone. The shorter man's features slackened, his eyes glazed over, and his body was dropped to the floor. Stefan bent down and pulled out the man's pockets, removed the bills that had been stuffed inside, half rolled him over and took a small leather wallet from his back pocket. He let the body roll back, backed away, and went rapidly down the hallway. He was at the door to the alley when he heard the bell from the elevator and the doors opening. He went outside, holding the door so that it would close silently, and walked down the cobblestones of the alley.

A large orange cat sat on the hood of a BMW parked near the entrance to the alley, and he reached over and stroked the soft fur of the animal, looking both ways down the street before emerging into the pedestrian traffic on the sidewalk.

Cardini went around to the front entrance of the hotel, entered, asked at the desk if he had any messages, and picked up an envelope sealed heavily with clear mailing tape. The name 'Joe Pelloni' was on the outside, with no return address.

"A man dropped this off for you about an hour ago. It was before I started working; the other clerk was here." The young desk clerk wore thick glasses with gold frames, and when he smiled, he had silver braces on his teeth fastened in with small pink dots of a substance that gave him an even more youthful look.

"Grazie." As Cardini turned away the telephone rang. He heard the clerk say "Pronto?" and launch into a rapid conversation in Italian.

His room was as he had left it, and he tossed his jacket on the bed. He put the envelope on the desk, slit the tape with his pocket knife, and he slid out the contents. Wrapped in plastic was a thick packet of euros. He would count it later. A separate white letter-sized envelope contained a single sheet of paper with an encrypted message. Cardini removed the small notebook from the inside pocket of his jacket, opened it to sheets of codes, and sat at the desk to decipher it.

So a company called Marsdon Security from the United States was providing some of the protection for participants in the meeting tomorrow. Verifying his previous investigation, the woman calling herself Elaine Birdsall was part of that operation, a contract employee used in covert operations. He smiled, remembering how he had nearly been duped by her cover. She was good, and he wondered about her actual identity. No matter. It would all be over by tomorrow, and he would be on his way. He had plans. She was only a woman. Obviously sent to keep an eye on him.

It would be good to look in the mirror and see Stefan again, to cast aside the 'Joe Pelloni' identity. Even the clothing he had selected was not his own, and felt uncomfortable. He preferred living in more tropical areas, wearing a pair of bathing trunks and a loose shirt and sandals. Northern areas always seemed to be the places he had to go for his work. The layers of clothing made him feel suffocated.

Killing was never a problem, however. It was just a job, and he was well paid. The euros in the envelope were only half of the amount that he would realize after tomorrow. His investments had paid handsomely, and after tomorrow would continue to do so.

The briefcase he had taken to the Vatican library was sitting on the floor next to the desk, and he pulled out the note pads on which he had scribbled notes. He used his cell phone camera to record the pages of writing, wadded up the pages, and tossed them in the wastebasket. The documents he had read were of interest to him. He would probably never publish the material. It had just been an exercise to cover his real objective. But perhaps after this last job, he could pursue his interests. The information would serve to enhance his weapons collection.

After a long hot shower and a change of clothes, he removed the contents of a black leather duffel bag that he would carry with him. It had strong shoulder straps and could be worn as a backpack or carried with one hand. He unwrapped the money and began separating it into smaller stacks that were then wrapped in the socks, underwear, shirts and pants. There was no metal involved, and with the identification that had been provided, he doubted the bag would be searched. Carry-on luggage was so plentiful these days that the inspectors at the airports were swamped with searches for metal objects and had a tendency to miss the soft things. There were, of course, dogs at some of the terminals sniffing for drugs, but he had none.

The black suit, shirt and white collar of a priest was hanging in the closet in a dry cleaner's bag. He tore open the bag. His cell phone, wallet and the small notebook would go in the pockets. He could carry the duffel bag, as there were many priests visiting the city from various parts of the world, especially for the meeting. After he had delivered his package and set the detonator, he could walk away, mix with the crowd at St. Peter's square, and disappear.

The briefcase next to the desk was also covered in black leather. He placed it on the bed and used a small screwdriver on his compact knife to remove the four small Phillips screws inside the lid of the case, and removed four more screws inside the case bottom. The false lid came out with a bit of prying, as did the false bottom. He laid the thin pieces of reinforced cardboard covered with black leather on the bed. The substance inside the case looked like a foam insulation material, but was actually a type of plastic explosive. It would act as a kind of pre-explosive detonator for the nuclear device that lay beneath it.

Cardini's assignments as a sniper had been assassination of individuals, but he had always wanted to use a weapon of this type. This was the first chance he had to actually do it. There was an element of excitement he never had experienced before, and he had to be careful not to let his enthusiasm make him careless.

The last part of the encrypted message gave him instructions to definitely eliminate the Elaine person if at all possible, but if not, go ahead as planned. It appeared that she was harmless, probably just there to check on him and report back. He had seen nothing to indicate otherwise. What could a woman do? Not much.

Working at the desk, he placed wires and the detonator into the foam-like substance. The wires came up the handle to the lock, which he dismantled. He inserted the wires into the lock with a small device that would explode unless the lock numbers were set a certain way. He decided to enter the devil's numbers 666 and then added an asterisk, appropriate for the explosion that would follow. A cell phone was then wired to both the top and bottom of the device, the panels replaced, and the phone placed inside the briefcase in a small leather pouch fastened to the case near the top opening.

The other cell phone that would call the one in the case would go in his pocket. The phones had already been programmed so that a single digit would set up a series of instructions culminating in first the explosion of the briefcase and its contents.

It was enough to eliminate the entire area of the Vatican not enough to eliminate the entire city of Rome. But it at least it was nuclear, and its effects would be felt for many, many years to come. It would be the culmination of his career. He had already made arrangements for quick transport out of the city, and would be miles away before any detonation took place. He closed the briefcase carefully.

Chapter 27- Safe House

The building was a three story gray brick structure similar to others on the cobbled street. A few steps up to a plain gray door. Shuttered windows on either side behind ornate gray painted iron gratings.

The door of the safe house closed behind her, and Alexi walked down the short, austere undecorated hallway behind the woman who had let her in. Pale tan carpet and pale cream walls. Institutional. No mirrors or pictures, only a narrow pale oak table along the right side of the hallway.

She wished she could just set her heavy shoulder bag down someplace. At the end of the hall was a heavy pale oak door

"Please come in here," the woman said. She was short and thin, wearing dark clothing. Her face nearly translucent with faint blue lines of veins along the sides of her forehead. Although she seemed fairly young, there were dark circles under her brown eyes. She wore no makeup and her clothing was dark and nondescript. Her lips were thin and pressed tightly together as she opened the heavy door.

Alexi followed her into a large room whose windows were shaded with a kind of translucent folded material. Dark brown carpeting accented with a scattering of bright patterned Oriental rugs. Light oak furniture. Two sofas covered in red leather facing each other on either side of a large coffee table. A fireplace at one end of the room covered with a copper screen perforated in a peacock design. Lamps with pierced copper shades on the oak tables at either end of the couches. Not like the safe houses she had stayed in on the other side of the pond, with their basics, pizza boxes and scuffed furniture.

"Make yourself comfortable. Can I get you something?" The woman stood with her arms folded around her waist, a position Alexi had seen some women use that had been in prison. Body language. No. Stop. Hold it. What had the woman asked?

"Yes, tea would be great!" She put her bag on one of the couches, and sank down into its soft luxury, smelling the richness of the leather.

The woman left the room by a door opposite the entry, and Alexi slipped her feet out of her shoes. Just knowing there was a locked door between her and the outside street - this place even *felt* safe.

She had nearly dozed off when the woman returned with her tea and a plate of small crisp cookies. "Oh, you were nearly asleep, I'm sorry!" She placed a fragile porcelain cup of tea with a matching saucer and a plate of tiny cookies on the coffee table.

Alexi sat up, slipped her feet back in her shoes and picked up the cup. It was hot but not so much that she couldn't drink it. The cookies smelled and tasted of almonds, and had tiny bits of nuts in them. The woman sat down opposite her on the other couch.

"You can call me Rachel. I live here and help take care of the visitors. They come and go. But there are three of us who are always here." Her speech was a careful and precise English like that learned in school. "You are to meet the others on your team as soon as you are rested. Your suitcase was taken up to your room. I will show you where it is. The meeting tonight is after dinner."

"Thank you. You are very kind, and I appreciate the hospitality." Alexi took another of the cookies, popped it in her mouth, and chewed. The last of the tea washed it down, and she placed the cup carefully on the saucer.

"So, if you are ready, we can go upstairs." Rachel stood up and Alexi followed her to the door that led into another hallway, a long flight of narrow stairs carpeted in the same tan as the front hallway. Same cream colored walls with a few oil paintings of famous places in Rome.

They passed three other doors; Rachel opened the fourth door on the right. Alexi's suitcase was on the floor next to the bed. The same folded blinds were over the windows, letting in light but with no view in or out. The bed was large and looked comfortable with a thick quilted spread and large pillows. A desk, chair and dresser were against the wall opposite the bed, and a night stand next to the bed held only a lamp. A small bathroom. Soft towels folded on a tier of shelves, along with bottles of toilet articles. Everything looked and felt safe.

"Very nice, Rachel. Thank you so much!" Alexi put her shoulder bag on the bed, and turned to smile at the small woman. "This means a lot to me right now." Did it? Alexi appreciated the relief she felt in the safe house, knowing there were others guarding its perimeters. Had she responded to Rachel so positively only because the woman seemed to need assurance? Did Alexi really belong in a safe house, when she was used to working alone?

Rachel returned her smile, her thin lips curling a bit, and small dimples appearing at the corners of her mouth. She hunched her shoulders a bit in a self-deprecating way, and then turned to leave. "Dinner is downstairs at six o'clock. The meeting is right after."

Alexi stripped off her clothes and stood under the hot shower for several minutes, feeling as though she were washing off layers of dirt. She didn't see a switch for a fan, so she swung the bathroom door back and forth a few times to air out the bathroom.

After another half hour spent drying her hair, stretching and doing a few exercises, applying a bit of makeup, she dressed in a comfortable pair of slacks and the soft rose-colored sweater she had worn to the airport in Detroit, and began to feel almost human again.

She took the cell phone out of her bag and dialed Neil in Ann Arbor.

"Roma here. Safe house."

"Yo. Good! About time! You okay?"

"Fine." She waited.

"Your target for sure is the Joe-guy."

"Yes, I know."

"You couldn't do him?"

"No. Problems. You were right. He's got associates. They tried to do me, but it didn't work out for them."

There was a silence on the other end. Then he spoke and his voice was the serious harsh sound she had learned to dread.

"That guy - the Kling-on that turned out to be not so good? Probably got hold of your info here. Not all, just the part about the contract for Rome. Nothing personal. Don't worry."

But she did worry. She had a life, a place. Her house. Chaz upstairs. She hoped she could trust Neil and the company.

"So now what?" She sat down on the bed, curling her toes tightly in the soft carpeting.

"The meeting there? So you go join the team. They've got a full heads-up, and they need you."

"I'm not a team player, Neil. I work alone."

"Not this time."

She sat for a minute. This wasn't what she had contracted to do, or what she had planned. She wasn't about guns; she was about disguised and lethal knitting needles. She could just walk away from a job and know that the cleaners would follow and take care of it, and she could go home.

"I don't like it, Neil."

"Yeah, I know. He just didn't turn out to be a senile old cougar, but part of a bunch of bad cats. He may be getting up there, but he sure as hell isn't ready for retirement."

"No shit." She thought of the 'Joe Pelloni' she had spent time with and the chill when he had taken her arm.

"Pelloni is *not* full of baloney, so you be careful. Be a team player now, got it?"

"I guess." She wasn't sure. Maybe she could make contact by herself. Maybe she could take the bastard out by herself.

"I'm not joking around here. You go with the team now. They're on protection detail, rooftop stuff. Need someone good with long-distance. You know him; you'll recognize him, even if he uses some kind of disguise. Be sharp. Help them out."

"All right." She still wasn't sure.

"We heard there could be some kind of nuclear device. Probably set with a timer, maybe small, but it could be damn lethal. Maybe blow up Rome itself, who knows?"

"Where did you get the intel on that?" She knew that Marsdon Security had many sources of information in its covert operation section.

"Can't tell you. Locked down intel."

"Oh." She still didn't feel comfortable working with a team. She didn't know these people.

"If he is successful, it will blow everything out of the water. No meeting to plan the conference - no conference. No Vatican - think what it will do to the Catholic church - the repercussions and fallout on a grand scale."

"Some of the radicals would be ecstatic."

"And a hell of a lot of them wouldn't be. They'd probably get blamed. Think about it. Remember - it looks like this is economically based, not religious."

"Yeah?"

"And 'Lexi - this would be the first nuclear device exploded in a city in how many years.....?"

"It could set a precedent...." Her voice was low now, and she shuddered to think of more of the devices used in other cities. If they could stop this one, this time...

"You're getting it. I had my doubts there...."

"Trying to sort out the two targets has been pretty confusing. And shaking your tail wasn't any picnic." She didn't mention her own inner doubts about the similarities between herself and Cardini.

"So who's paying the company for all this? The Feds?" She had never asked before. Thinking about potential economic purposes of the upcoming council, she still wondered. Most smaller countries beset with civil wars and insurgencies had been experiencing tribal and religious warfare for hundreds if not thousands of years. Few of them had the resources to pay the kind of money she knew it was taking to mount a protection team. Only the more affluent governments could afford to set up contracts, and governments were running on empty.

"Not this time. I shouldn't be telling you this, but it's corporate. A group, mainly food distributors, oil companies, the ones that want to set up manufacturing in places that have been inaccessible."

"I see." Alexi could see CHEAP LABOR like a neon sign in her mind. Business as usual. Calm down the natives, buy off the locals with low-paying jobs, pay off the chieftains under the table. Milk the country of its resources through mining and oil wells. Set up a so-called democratic government of puppets who would do as they were told.

She could feel the tea and cookies rising at the back of her throat. Was this any different than the arms and biochemical manufacturers and dealers? It was all about making a profit. Avoiding the labor unions. Just putting more money in the pockets of those who already had more than enough. Giving a pittance to the ones who worked all their lives. She felt sick.

Neil didn't say anything. He waited.

"I'll have to think about it, Neil. I'll call you after the meeting." She shut down the cell phone and sat on the edge of the bed. It was nearly time to go to dinner.

She picked through her shoulder bag, removed non-essential items and left them in the suitcase. Everything she really needed was in the bag. She could just walk out the front door. Find Cardini with the tracker.

Patriot? Yeah, right. More like a corporate flunky. Shit. How many times had it been like this before? Had she killed someone just so that life could go on as usual for people she would never meet? Was she just a tool - another one of the 'unwashed masses?'

Kill or be killed. Maybe the mime with a gun was just the beginning. Was she on someone's shit list now? Was she herself now a target? Cardini must have made her, but he wasn't acting alone. She felt cold. Her fingers on the strap of the shoulder bag tightened.

Alexi walked stiffly down the stairs toward the sound of voices. Might as well eat first. Then like the song – she could just 'slip out the back, Jack.'

Chapter 28 - The team – the purpose

A few of the faces in the group of people standing around talking in the dining room looked familiar. Four of the men she had never seen--tall rugged types with broad shoulders and a military aura, probably mercenaries who opted for higher pay with a private contractor. Two were talking to each other in French, and the others in English. Quite a few wore loose shirts and tops that only partially concealed hand guns or other weapons.

Alexi saw one woman she had met before – cleaner - sitting at the table, her dark hair caught back in a barrette, talking to another woman that Alexi had never seen, and their conversation sounded like Hebrew. Probably originally Mossad. The babble of voices was kept low, but was definitely multi-lingual.

The woman with the powder-horn purse who had introduced herself as Elli was sitting with a man with dark hair, talking seriously. She looked up at Alexi, gave her a little wave of recognition and went back to their conversation.

Rachel came into the dining room carrying two steaming casseroles followed by a gangly young boy that balanced a platter of hot vegetables. There were already platters with antipasto on the table, and baskets of crusty bread. A glass and a bottle of water had been placed at each table setting. As the food was deposited, the people in the room found chairs, sat down, and began passing and reaching for the food, piling their plates without ceasing their conversations.

Alexi sat in a chair next to the woman who had been dressed as a gypsy. She picked up a napkin and placed it on her lap.

"Oh, hi!" The beautiful woman turned to her, a broad smile on her face. "So glad you finally made it!" She seemed genuine. The extra cell phone with the rubber band was still somewhere in her bag, but she had never used it.

"Oh, yes. Here I am." Alexi reached for a piece of bread. She still felt deep resentment at having to join the team and wished she had simply made a move on Cardini at the Pantheon. The liquid in the tiny syringe would have done the job, and she wouldn't have to be here. Far too many people in the room. She couldn't imagine herself working with them on anything.

"Sam will be here soon, he'll fill us in about tomorrow."

"So what is your name - Donna? Or....."

"Actually it isn't Donna - it's Madonna. And I do have a last name - it's De Medici." She grinned. "No shit."

Alexi thought she was being put on, but went along with it. "Right."

"For real. Madonna De Medici."

"Are you related to...."

"Absolutely."

"I suppose you have those little poison lockets for emergencies." Alexi grabbed an olive from the antipasto.

Madonna reached in the neck of her blouse, pulled out a silver necklace with a fat oval locket dangling from it. "None other."

"Locked and loaded?" Alexi took another olive, a big green one this time with a huge pit. She scraped her teeth down it, enjoying the salty bitter flavor.

"Right on." Madonna grinned, lifting her eyebrows and wiggling them, trying to appear evil but not quite pulling it off.

Alexi laughed and felt herself begin to relax. "Does that mean I'd better watch my food if I'm sitting next to you?"

"I doubt it." Madonna opened the locket and it revealed pictures of two small children. "My kids - Sean and Cindy."

"Wow. Cute kids. Where are they?"

"With their dad in Toledo. We live there. I do contract work sometimes, used to work with the feds, but when the kids came along, decided to just work part time."

Alexi didn't ask what Madonna had done for the feds, but she suspected it was the same kind of covert work that others in the room had been doing. Although she worked alone, she knew there must be others. She had few opportunities to see anyone but Daniel, Neil and a couple of the secretaries in the office.

The door to the dining room opened and the man she suspected was Sam walked in. His dark hair and moustache streaked with gray were the same as when he posed as a gypsy, evidently real. But who and what was real? He walked quickly to the head of the table, took a plate from the place setting and walked around behind people, reaching between them to fill his plate with food. He moved as though on roller blades, incredibly graceful as he talked and scooped up helpings, avoiding long conversations. Going back to the head of the table, he unscrewed the top of the water bottle, tipped it up and took a long drink.

"We can talk while we eat if that's all right with you." His voice carried to the other end of the long table, conversations died, and everyone looked toward him.

"For those who don't know me, I'm Sam Westin, with Marsdon Security. As you know, this is a contract job to provide protection for the representatives from various countries who will be attending the planning meeting tomorrow. This is crucial in that it sets the agenda for a conference that it is hoped will bring an end or at least a cessation of some of the violence that has been harming millions of people for far too long." He paused to take a bite of food, chewed and swallowed. Others at the table picked up their forks and began eating, keeping their eyes on him.

"Now." He swallowed again, and took a sip of water from the bottle. "We need to meet each other, and we need to trust each other. Since most of us are not that well acquainted and probably will not see each other again, that will be a challenge. Especially considering the kinds of work we do and the fact that many of us are used to working either alone or in very small groups."

What followed was a compressed version of getting acquainted and building trust conducted by Sam and Madonna. Alexi was at first skeptical, then felt her defenses coming down, and by the end of that part of the evening, she had not only eaten her dinner but had memorized the names of everyone on the team, heard them give thumbnail sketches of their past work for Marsdon Security, and began to feel a small sense of trust with the group.

The language used was English, so the babble of languages was gone. Each of the members stated clearly their areas of expertise, and she realized that each person had several years, if not decades, of experience in covert operations.

The main duty of the team was to provide protection for the representatives from various countries as they shifted from their hotel, across St. Peter's square, and into a side entrance to the Vatican. Once inside the Vatican, the Swiss Guards were in charge, well prepared to provide protection. Outside the buildings, there were guards and local police, but Marsdon Security was charged with not only locating the person or persons who were most likely to sabotage the meeting, but to take them out with impunity, on the spot.

"It is most probable that there is a small suitcase type nuclear bomb that will be brought into the square and detonated, and that a well-known assassin – Stefan Cardini - called the Cougar will be carrying it and some kind of detonation device, possibly a cell phone which he could use either in the square as a suicide bomber, or after he gets far enough away from the bomb to escape without harm to himself. We doubt that he is suicidal.

"From the intelligence we have received, the bomb is large enough to completely destroy the Vatican and possibly Rome itself if it is detonated. We don't believe that it is a device capable of greater destruction, but as you know the fallout and years of devastation that could follow would be horrible. It also could trigger the beginning of nuclear attacks in other places."

Alexi was the one who had been closest to the one called the Cougar, and she was expected to identify him for the snipers and others on the ground.

"We will be placing many of the team on the roofs overlooking the square, and Alexi; we want you there as well. You will all be given appropriate long range weapons with telescopic lenses. Alexi - when you identify the man we suspect is carrying the device, just speak into the microphone to alert the team. There will be others on the ground in the square, and you will all be able to contact each other. We need to practice using the microphones, so let's get started."

Madonna went to a cabinet and took out a large plastic tub with small boxes containing communications gear. She went around the table and gave each person a box. Alexi opened hers and found a small earphone and a tiny microphone that could be clipped to her shirt. Looking around, she saw others placing the earphones and microphones. They were nearly invisible once in place. There was no way to adjust the volume, but when Madonna spoke into her microphone in a normal voice, the earphone picked up the sound. She then whispered so that she could not be heard a few feet away. The sound was still very clear.

Madonna began moving silverware and dishes on the table, and although Alexi could hear it with her other ear, the one with the earphone did not pick up the sounds. Madonna instructed them to cover the ear without the earphone, and Alexi could then only hear Madonna speaking. The earphone completely blocked out all other noise. Madonna showed them the small earplugs that could be used in their other ear to make it possible to hear team members but warned them that it would also block out anyone else speaking to them.

Sam went out of the room with two of the men. They came back carrying boxes of long-range rifles, small handguns, and enough cartridges to supply everyone with an abundance of ammo. Team members who would be posted to the rooftops were given the rifles with telescopic sights. Alexi received one of those rifles, and a box of cartridges. She didn't mention the gun and cartridges already in her bag...

At the end of the room, Madonna pulled down a screen and Sam showed maps of the area, placement of team members, and gave assignments. He repeated the information and asked for questions. Madonna sat down at the table, and looked around the room at the team members, encouraging them to bring up anything of concern. No one spoke.

Madonna brought Alexi a newer type of light-weight rifle with long-range capability that shot hollow-point bullets. For a trained sniper, the chances of collateral damage to innocent bystanders were diminished. The hollow-points would explode inside the target on impact.

The rest of the team had heavier guns whose weight alone would be improbable for her. Accepting that fact, she loaded the shells as shown and set the safety. Her suitcase was still in her room. Everything she really needed was in her bag. Things in the suitcase could be replaced. Cardini was probably at the Trevi. She could just walk out the door, wrap the rifle in her jacket or leave it behind?

The assignments and team placements were reviewed again. Alexi held the rifle upright next to her and placed the cartridges in her bag. She had used this same rifle on the practice range many times. It would make her job easier, and it put a distance between her and Joe Baloney. She had almost been attracted to him. If she had to look in his eyes would she hesitate? This way, it wouldn't happen. Perhaps she could go along with the team. She had been perched on the edge of her chair, but now slid back.

The talk with Neil had unnerved her, however, and she wished there was some way she could justify what she was doing - if it was only to make some billionaire even more wealthy, she was in the wrong business.

It was as though Sam could read her thoughts. "Okay, everyone. I pulled this together just to remind us of the alternatives. If we don't get this guy, this is what can happen. In case you feel a moment's hesitation, think of this."

Madonna started up another presentation with pictures and quiet statements about What Is - the refugee camps, bodies lying on the ground without arms and legs, decapitations, raped women, piles of stripped bodies and devastated homes. The pictures went by rapidly, one after the other of the violence and horror that people inflicted on other people.

Then she showed the devastation after Nagasaki, the horrors of that nuclear weapon so long ago. Again, picture after picture that Alexi had seen before, but not for many years. It was so easy to forget.

Finally, she showed pictures of What Could Be - people living in small homes, working at perhaps menial jobs, but sufficient to meet their needs. Children going to school in different countries, some in buildings with no walls, only thatched roofs, others with plain but clean rooms filled with children who were whole. There were pictures of factories with people working at machines or making things by hand.

"These people are in peaceful countries that are exploited by big business interests, and work for low wages. But they are not being murdered. The companies that hire them do not give them adequate benefits, but they do not kill them or cut off their arms and legs. It will be many years before they form unions and demand higher wages and benefits. For now, it's enough to simply be left alone to work and live without fear. Of course, there are still factions in those countries who have differing political and religious beliefs, and there is trouble, but with adequate protection, no outright civil wars. Some of them are beginning to have adequate education programs and health care."

Madonna showed pictures of the puppet rulers of two of the countries, bought and paid for by corporations and administrations of the super-powers. They were smiling, and their homes and cars were large. They were shown with powerful and famous people, standing and smiling for the cameras. For this, she didn't have to speak. Everyone in the room knew what was being displayed.

Then she showed pictures of the dictators, their massive pictures proclaiming power, their armies and militias, the devastation they wrought, the refugees and the piles of bodies. The presentation had gone full circle. She had made her point.

Sam spoke quietly. "The world is not perfect. The people who pay us are not perfect. The world they want to create and perpetuate is not perfect. We are not perfect. Some of them will profit greatly from the work we do to keep this meeting and the conference alive. Those who supply food and products for a peaceful existence will become even richer. We can do nothing about that. But the alternative is more of the devastation and corruption that makes millions of people's lives unbearable."

Madonna spoke up. "There are no good guys and bad guys. But we seem to be working for the least destructive."

Alexi felt numb. She heard others talking as though she were in a long tunnel and they were at the other end. She wanted to get away from these people. She stood up, picked up her rifle and bag, and went to the door. Madonna and the others began collecting their belongings.

They would meet in the morning for breakfast in the dining room and leave for the Vatican. Alexi was exhausted. She would stay. She just wanted to go to her room. By this time tomorrow they would either be successful or they would all be part of the dust left behind from the detonation of a nuclear bomb.

Chapter 29 - To the Vatican.

Alexi woke to the sound of a knock on her door. She got ready to go downstairs, removed everything from her suitcase that she absolutely needed and put it in her backpack.

The team was assembled in the dining room. Rachel and other members of the staff had prepared a buffet breakfast. She sat next to the woman from Toledo, but they spoke very little.

Each member of the rooftop sniper Upper Team had brought a rifle and backpack. Sam and Madonna brought out a carton full of long dark sports type duffel bags for the rifles and handed out gray jackets.

Alexi still felt like leaving the team. All she had to do was walk out the door. Her suitcase was still in her room, but everything she really needed was in her bag. The things in the suitcase could be replaced.

The Lower Team people wore casual tourist clothing with bulky light jackets to hide bullet-proof vests under their shirts. They would be in St. Peter's square attempting to spot the assassin or assassins.

"Listen up, everyone," said Sam. His voice carried well in the suddenly silent room. Madonna stood a bit behind him, only her eyes moving as she watched the reactions of team members while they listened.

The plan was simple, and the review brief. Access to the rooftops was already arranged with the Swiss Guards and Vatican security administration. The Upper Team would take a stairway used by Vatican staff, and the Lower Team would be positioned around the square.

The two-way microphones were checked, with Sam and Madonna going around the room making sure everyone was connected. Individuals were to identify themselves with codes - Upper One for the first team member on the rooftop, Upper Two for the team person next down the line. Alexi was Upper Six.

Lower One was the first team member in the square, and so on. Codes for various situations were repeated several times by the entire group in a kind of mantra, to make sure they were memorized.

Target One was Cardini. Alexi felt a surge of slight nausea remembering the charm and attraction she had felt toward him. Disgust with her own gullibility was dispelled by remembering her earlier caution in dealing with him.

"Please update his location, Alexi," said Sam.

She checked her cell ap tracker. No movement. "He's still at his hotel."

Sam nodded and continued the briefing. Any associate of Cardeni - would be called Target Two. Sam's expression changed from the matter-of-fact, business-as-usual to a grim pulling down of the corners of his mouth coupled with a slight lifting of his chin.

"Remember that this is a potential incident with severe long-term effects if we are unable to stop it. Once a single nuclear device is detonated, it could trigger a wave of such incidents in many other places. It is not the destruction of the Vatican complex itself. Churches have been burnt before, and raised from the ashes. Even Popes can be replaced." He stopped then, and looked around the room, finding the eyes of every member of the team before speaking again.

"We expected an aging sniper that was misguided, perhaps senile. Covert operations were in place to deter that person from acting unwisely now or in the future." Sam looked at Alexi then and gave her a wry half-smile. "But things changed. In receiving intel about the real plan and the nuclear device, and didn't have much time to assemble this team. Everything has been moving pretty fast."

Alexi wondered how the intel had been obtained, and whether Sam and Madonna were actually employees of Marsdon Security, or covert operatives with the federal government. She would save that question for later, if any of them were still around.

Sam continued: "If you have any qualms about simply taking out a target, let me know right now, and you will be relieved of duty." He waited, and there was no sound in the room. Madonna stood next to him looking around the room.

Alexi straightened her back, slid back in the chair, rotated her shoulders slightly and took in a deep breath. No problem. Ready.

The group collected their gear and went out a back entrance to a tour bus with darkened windows. Alexi squeezed into one of the back seats with her gear, the bag with the assault rifle pressed into her hip next to the window, shoulder bag on the floor between her feet.

Like others in the Upper Team, she was dressed in dark gray clothing, with a reversible t-shirt underneath that could be changed to a light color in order to blend in with tourists if necessary. On the roof, her hair and face would be covered with a thin dark gray balaclava cap so that it didn't reflect sunlight. Thin dark gray gloves would cover the hands of the team members on the rooftops, also to prevent reflection and draw any attention to them from below. The guns were a matte grey, and would blend in with the darkened stone at the edges of the rooftops.

They arrived at a side entrance and were escorted inside quickly by Vatican security staff in dark suits. The door closed behind them quietly, guarded by two Swiss Guards in tan uniforms holding assault rifles. The narrow stone spiral staircase to the roof was not an easy climb. Her shoulder bag heavy with ammo and the duffel bag with the rifle. She could just keep up with the younger team members. She wished she had been more enthusiastic about her exercise regimen.

The team made their way down a short hallway to a plain metal door opened by another uniformed Vatican guard, and walked out onto the sunlit expanse of the stone rooftop. The sky above was blue with only a scattering of small clouds. Early morning sunlight laid long shadows across the rooftop from the shoulder-high wall around the periphery. The wall was thick and plain from the back, carved on the exterior face which would help hide the snipers positioned behind the thick stone. Stone statues rose above the wall at intervals. Alexi let her duffel bag drop to the ground for a moment as she surveyed the area. Sam was directing Upper Team members to their positions.

Two of the men had carried the larger duffel bags with heavier long-range rifles to the roof and began handing them out. Alexi had carried her own rifle, plus the heavy shoulder bag. She thought about how she had worried that she might slow down the others and smiled. She had been carrying a heavier load than some of them, that was all. Probably thought too much about getting old.

Built in a medieval style with slots for archers, the wall had incorporated the defense aspects of its construction into its decoration. Placed at the same distances, ancient archers would have been standing with crossbows. The team members were primarily hidden from view, but could sight out the openings down to St. Peter's square.

Alexi took the place assigned her, and peered through the long rectangular opening to the area below. The mass of folding chairs was visible, divided into sections, beginning to fill with people. She only had a view of a segment of them, and the ability to see any of the area behind the chairs was restricted. She moved to her left, to a wider opening in the ornate wall, looked over the edge somewhat, and had a broader view. The meeting representatives would be coming across the area behind the chairs, and if there was an attack on them it would be there.

Speaking into her mic, she said "Upper Six here. View through slot too restrictive."

Sam's voice came back: "Roger. Use whatever works." He had now gone down to the Lower team and was somewhere in the square.

She saw others move between the rectangular archer's slots and the openings in the ornate wall, removing rifles from their duffel bags, inserting cartridges, and sighting the weapons. She followed their lead.

Some members of the Upper Team were already sitting on the stones of the rooftop, leaning against the surrounding wall, sipping from canteens.

Again, she thought of Joe Baloney - how she had nearly been suckered in with his charm. She wondered what he was thinking right now, how he could justify his actions. If he was actually carrying some kind of nuclear device, what significance it could possibly have for him. How he thought he could get far enough away before it detonated. Or was he planning some kind of suicide attack? Having met him, she doubted that he was a suicide bomber. But surely the man must realize the significance of such an action... or did he? He must only care about himself.

She checked her tracker. "He's moving. Coming this way."

Alexi pulled the balaclava out of one pocket, the thin gloves out of the other and put them on. She thought about her old rationale for 'taking out old men.' Patriotism. But like everything else, it all came down to the old word Greed. That's the way the world worked, and she was only a small part of it.

Remembering the previous times she had 'taken out' the old demented assassins - the rush of pleasure that the simple act of vengeance had given her just knowing she could do it. Alexi wondered for an instant whether it was something innate in her that hungered for excitement. Perhaps she was really at heart just a killer.

Pushing internal thoughts out of her mind, she checked the tracker again. "He's close."

Sam's voice in her ear cut through the thoughts. "Listen up. Lower Team on alert. Tour bus arriving with participants." Alexi and the other team members stood up and looked over the wall carefully, not revealing their positions.

She looked down to the area where the tour busses were angled into parking places and saw a long black bus with darkened windows come to a stop. Tan uniformed Swiss Guards were already moving toward the bus, looking anything but unobtrusive although they weren't dressed as ornately as their compadres.

Men and women began leaving the bus carrying briefcases and notebooks. Most were in business attire, but a few wore the flowing robes, keffiya and hijab head coverings. They were not talking among themselves, and moved quickly, apparently aware of the possibility of some kind of attack. Some were hunched over as though they expected something violent. Others just walked rapidly, looking straight ahead. Guards alongside them, they moved toward the entrance into the Vatican.

Alexi scanned the area through her scope. No sign of Cardini. Her tracker showed that he was still a short distance away.

She heard Lower Team members in her earpiece murmuring to Sam and each other. Nothing unexpected so far. Tourists and locals were still coming into the square, taking seats in the mass of folding chairs set up for the papal message and blessing. The vendors had set up their tables around the periphery, some with small awnings to shade them from the sun. It was still a bit early for the walking vendors with their trinkets and souvenirs, but one dark African man had begun offering bright colored scarves to the tourists.

Now the participants for the meeting were at the heavily guarded doorway, going inside the building. It had only taken a few moments. Nothing had happened. Alexi swung the telescopic lens back and forth around the moving line of people entering the square, up and down the persons sitting on the chairs. No one that looked like Cardeni.

She checked the tracker. "He's here."

Sam's voice came through as though he was standing next to her, and she lowered the rifle and sight. "He's in. Stay alert. Go to Phase Two."

The search now for Cardeni and any possible carrying case for a device was the focus of both teams. Alexi stood the rifle next to her against the wall, took binoculars from her pocket and began to scan the people below. Other tour busses were pulling into the parking area, disgorging people unaware of the drama being played out around them. Maintaining focus, not being distracted by the activities in the square that revolved around the Pope's appearance was essential for every member of the team.

The number of priests and nuns in the square was increasing. Some were arriving on foot, and others came out of the Vatican buildings. Others came on tour busses, moving toward the seats in groups. The priests were primarily dressed in suits, only their collars indicating their profession. Some, however, wore long skirts that flapped about their legs as they walked. The nuns appeared to be wearing a variety of clothing, representing the order to which they belonged. There were also the brothers who represented various orders, some in long skirted robes and others in suits. Many were carrying bags of different shapes and sizes, as were the tourists and locals.

Although everyone had to present themselves and their ticket at the check-in table manned by a young priest, and there were Vatican guards keeping a watchful eye on everyone going into the square, none of the purses, bags, backpacks or other things people were carrying were being inspected. Alexi felt a cold chill run down her spine. In an attempt to avoid panic, deal with the huge number of people in a short time, and protect the privacy of religious followers, a serious breach of security was happening.

She adjusted the binoculars so that she could see the faces of the people below clearly, making sure that she covered everyone moving toward the chairs before they were seated. She was positioned to have the best view of the square. since she was the only one who knew what Stefan Cardeni looked like, and reported in her mic as she cleared each area below.

A tour bus arrived and a group of Red Hat ladies poured out of the doors, their bright hats and boas making them stand out against the dark clothing of the religious types. It was the same group she had used to avoid the Kling-on. They seemed more subdued than when Alexi had seen them previously, and she watched through her binoculars as they followed Veronica to chairs in the area closest to the building where Alexi and her team of snipers were positioned.

The group of women were talking among themselves, and took some time getting seated. The papal message and blessing would begin soon. She saw Veronica collect shopping bags from other women and pile them up on the chair next to her.

Alexi made sure that she looked at each of the faces of the Red Hat ladies the same as others below. No one looked suspicious and she recognized most of them. She moved the binoculars and concentrated on others in that section.

As the area toward the front filled up, she called in her report. "Upper Six, first quarter clear." Where was Cardini? Red hats and dark hair dominated the area. No white haired man. A few bald ones, and women with white hair. Wait. There was one. She adjusted the binoculars. No. Not Cardini. He had to be there. Somewhere.

Chapter 30 - Decision.

At least a thousand of people had entered St. Peter's Square below and nearly filled the seats in preparation for the Pope's appearance. Alexi kept her attention on the faces, reminding herself that Stefan Cardeni was a master of disguise. She remembered how he walked and moved. He could be wearing a dark wig, perhaps some kind of artificial facial hair.

Then she saw a dark haired priest wearing a dark suit with a white collar carrying a thick dark briefcase. He walked slowly up the right hand aisle closest to Alexi, stopped and made his way to a chair at the end of the row. The row of Red Hat ladies. Only the chair with all the shopping bags separated him from Veronica. Alexi focused her binoculars on their faces and caught her breath. Stefan Cardeni.

"It's him. I've got him." She gave the location.

His handsome face was turned for just an instant, and she saw the familiar lines going from the sides of his nose to his mouth. She focused the lens sharply, bringing his face even closer. Yes. "Upper Six. Target identified. Priest, suit with collar. Dark hair, no hat. Midway right side at the end of the row with the Red Hat ladies. Thick dark briefcase."

"Roger." Sam responded. She heard him give instructions to the Lower team to move slowly toward the 'priest' in order to remove him from the area as unobtrusively as possible.

Stefan Cardeni placed a duffel bag under his seat and the briefcase between his chair and the one next to it. Veronica turned her head and said something to Cardeni. Alexi saw him look over and smile.

Sam's voice in her earpiece was clear, and the tension palpable. "Move with extreme caution. Do not approach. Wait for my signal. Try to prevent collateral damage."

Cardeni must have set the nuclear device so that he had enough time to get as far away as possible before it detonated. No way was he a suicide bomber. There would be no benefit in clearing the square, as the device would take out the entire Vatican anyway. It was up to the teams to remove both Cardeni and the device safely.

She put the binoculars in her pocket and picked up the assault rifle that leaned against the stone wall, sighting in on Cardeni with the telescopic lens. Her heart was now pounding and she had to take in another deep breath to calm herself.

The Lower Team was moving in toward him, and Alexi saw the team members position themselves within a few yards of Cardini. More people were filling in the center section of chairs now, behind the area where he was sitting. The rows were filling quickly. The chair next to Cardeni was still loaded with Red Hat ladies bags.

She watched him through the telescopic lens, realizing that she couldn't see both his face and his hands at the same time. He sat straight, his back rigid. He turned again to speak to Veronica.

Cardeni reached in his jacket pocket, and took out a small object. Alexi focused on it – a cell phone. Her heart leaped and she sucked in a breath. He spoke into it and returned it to his pocket. Contacting someone who would pick him up and get him as far away as fast as possible? Leave the case and detonate it once he was out of range.

Alexi put the rifle back against the wall in front of her. She grabbed her bag and walked quickly to the stairwell. There would be collateral damage if the team approach was used, and chaos in the square. People would get hurt, perhaps killed - innocent people who were there to be cured, not part of some melee between forces larger than themselves. She opened the door to the short hallway, letting it close behind her.

She moved down the stairs quickly, pulled off the gloves and balaclava. Dug the red hat out of her shoulder bag. By the time she had reached the bottom of the stairs, she had removed the gray jacket and dropped it, slid her own jacket out of the bag, and shoved her arms through it. Over the black top and slacks, with the silly red hat, she was more believable as a sweet little old lady.

Before she opened the door to the square, she checked the needles in the sleeves. She pulled out the earpiece and shoved it in her pocket. Opening the door, she drew confused looks from the guards standing on either side of the doorway, and stepped outside.

Alexi moved quickly to the aisle where Cardeni and the Red Hat ladies were sitting. "Oh, Veronica! You saved me the seat! Thanks!"

The woman looked up surprised, and a bit grudgingly removed the shopping bags and handed them down the row to their owners. Alexi smiled and waved at the other ladies. "Sorry I'm late."

She turned and smiled at Cardeni. The case was now between their chairs. His face registered surprise. Then anger.

Stefan Cardeni stood up, looked around and saw the Lower Team members coming toward them. He glared down at her, his handsome face distorted with hatred. People in the area looked at the unfolding action curiously.

Alexi stood up, facing Cardeni for an instant. "Oh, it's you! I didn't know you were a priest!"

She reached out toward him, one of the needles in her hand now. As though she were tripping, she let one knee collapse, and fell slightly toward him. Automatically, he reached out to prevent her fall. She heard the familiar 'Kudoz' in her mind and jabbed the needle into his arm through the black cloth.

His eyes were wide now, and he said nothing, but the effects of the narcotic were immediate, and he slumped down, half falling into his chair. Alexi bent over him and used her other hand with its needle to make the second thrust, hidden as a solicitous gesture of concern.

"Goodbye, Joe Baloney," she said under her breath as he slid from the chair to the pavement. The familiar rush of satisfaction and pleasure ran through her. It passed in an instant and she repressed her urge to let out a rebel yell.

Standing up, she saw the Lower Team members coming toward her, and heard the excited voices of the Red Hat ladies behind her.

"Oh my goodness! Help! Someone!" she said, waving her hands as though about to faint herself. In the seconds that followed, Alexi took in a breath and let it out slowly, a low steady hum coming from her throat that told her she was in complete control.

The Lower Team members rushed in as though to help the fallen priest. His body was completely limp now, and Alexi knew it would only be seconds before his heart would stop completely.

Team members who had been assigned to the nuclear device itself came in to move chairs and people away from it, making it look as though they were collecting the priest's case as a solicitous act. They also retrieved the cell phone from his pocket. Prearranged 'Paramedics' came quickly, placed Cardeni's body on a gurney and rushed it out of the square to a waiting ambulance. Alexi had already slid the now empty needles back into her sleeves.

"Well, that's enough excitement for the day! That poor man." The woman smiled over at Alexi. "Weren't you blonde? Was that a wig?"

"Caught me. My backup wig." Alexi grimaced but remained standing. People did notice things like that. Change the subject. Fast. "My goodness, wasn't that terrible? But they certainly are efficient here, aren't they?"

She waited until Veronica turned to talk to the woman in a large purple hat on her other side and picked up her backpack. She was still wearing the red hat, but didn't want to subject herself to any questions. Her heart was going just a bit fast, and she took another deep breath. For the next few minutes the Lower Team members would be involved with Cardeni. A perfect time to leave.

The ceremony in the square was about to begin. Alexi walked quickly to the street. The only thing back at the safe house was her suitcase. It would catch up with her or it wouldn't. She had everything important in her shoulder bag. Her knitting. The blue blouse. Chaz' little Harley. The small wooden box. Dumping the gun and shells could be done at the airport.

The taxi sped out of Rome. Alexi sat with her arms wrapped around her backpack. She felt relief. Time to go home. It had been a mistake to work with a team and she hoped she never had to do it again. The team approach was wrong for her. Sure, she needed others for intel. Being able to be in the right place at the right time probably had meant that she had to be up on that roof. Hopefully it was one of those single events that would never recur. It was over.

The pictures in Alexi's mind would recede, as did all the others. This time, there had been more at stake. But her insights would stay with her. Too tired now to think about it.

Her bank account would also experience a sharp increase. There were millions in the account now. How much money did she really need? She had already made enough.

Then she thought about how she had killed both of the white-haired men - yet right now, she felt nothing. Was this what it meant to have lived this long? To feel nothing? Or had killing become just a job to her? Nothing about her own life had changed - nothing exterior.

Remembering her attraction to Cardini and her tears after helping Jim escape the inevitable, she realized that she was able to feel something. Even though her body was aging and occasionally complaining, she still functioned physically, and the scars around her heart were perhaps not as thick as she had thought. There was Simon back home that said he loved her but she always kept him at arm's length. Well, not quite that far, but...

Epilogue – Three days later

The miniature motorcycle gift for Chaz waited on a table near her front door in a small bright bag with matching tissue paper. The small painting had been framed and hung on the wall in her dining room. Alexi sat in her chair in the living room, knitting basket beside her, watching a TV report on the promising results of the planning meeting for the upcoming ecumenical conference. No mention was made of the incident at St. Peter's square, or of any nuclear device.

Neil had filled her in on details by phone at the airport in Amsterdam. The Marsdon Security team had examined the nuclear device and the bomb squad moved it by helicopter to a small boat already waiting off the coast of Italy. It was smaller than expected. The device was dismantled and destroyed safely.

Alexi turned off the television and went to her computer and sent an anonymous donation from her account to the same organization Jim Russell had selected for his donation – the amount he had set aside for her as executor. The transfer of funds in New York had gone without incident, taking only a day in the city to carry out Jim's wishes. The empty small wooden box sat on her desk, a mute reminder of a morning on the Palatine, and a white-haired man.

She e-mailed Simon. "Hi. I'm back home. Any chance of getting together? Give me a call." Thought about the beginning of feelings for the handsome Cougar in Rome. Was she attracted to danger? A man like that always meant trouble. Simon was predictable, dependable, warm and comfortable. Not that exciting. Pretty good in bed, though. Alexi sighed.

Back in the living room she watched another newscast. A new production plant was opening in a country previously devastated by wars. The new president was meeting with a large industrialist at the country estate of the previous dictator. Flags were flying; smiling men rode in a golf cart. Pictures flashed quickly. Inside a new plant with rows of machines manned by local people. A new McDonalds had opened nearby, and a Wal-Mart was being built. No evidence of any of the traditional culture of the people. A schoolroom with adults learning the English language. Priests at a new church filled with parishioners.

Alexi remembered the small country before their civil war, the songs and dances of the people in traditional clothing - the rich heritage and culture that had existed. She wondered about their spiritual leaders, exquisite traditional arts and crafts, and a healthy and nutritious traditional diet. Would that exist now? Probably in the memories of elders, brought out on holidays - like many of the traditions of indigenous people all over the globe. Even the Arctic people couldn't get along without their snowmobiles. Internet and cell phones were a part of life in every country. But at least the people were alive.

She flipped off the television, picked up a bright red straw hat, put it in her worn bag, and headed for the door. A local group of Red Hat ladies were meeting at the Senior Center raising donations for the Cancer Fund.

Tomorrow she was leaving for the Orkney Islands. They had incredible knitters, wonderful wool yarn, and new patterns to learn. A real vacation.

Her cell phone began ringing as she walked down the outside steps to her car, and she looked at the caller ID. Neil again. He had tried to contact her three times that day already, but she just wasn't ready to take on another job. Not yet.

25734575R10090

Made in the USA
Lexington, KY
02 September 2013